Embracing The Unexpected

Book 1 of The Unexpected Series

by London St. Charles

LS Charles Publishing Group
Chicago, Illinois

LS Charles Publishing Group

www.londonstcharles.com

Embracing the Unexpected by London St. Charles

Copyright ©2021

Trade Paperback ISBN: 978-1-954498-99-0

E-Book ISBN: 978-0-9993288-6-6

Cover & Interior Design:

Gisele Marie www.authorgiselemarie.com

Editorial Consultant:

MarZé Scott www.marzescott.com

Dedication

"Appreciate a good man. If you have a good man, respect him,
honor him, and cherish him. You'll know he's a good man
because he's already doing those things for you.
Don't take him for granted."
—Tony Gaskins

To all the good men holding it down, I appreciate you!
—London St. Charles

Acknowledgments

Praises to The Almighty for bestowing the gift of writing in me, and for guiding me in my literary journey.

A secluded romantic cabin in the woods in Sevierville Tennessee was the inspiration for Embracing the Unexpected. My hubby and I rented the cabin I wrote about for our 15th anniversary getaway. The online images of the inside and the grounds were breathtaking, and I told my husband I was going to write a story based on the cabin. Two weeks before we were supposed to go, the Mayor of Chicago included Tennessee in a COVID-19 travel band, and we would have to quarantine for two weeks once we returned home. I had just reopened my daycare and I couldn't put the children at risk, so we rented a cabin along the riverbank in another state that wasn't on the list. We had the most amazing time, one that I'm still smiling about months later. However, the cabin in Tennessee continued to beckon me to pen its story, so here we are.

I want to thank everyone who played a role in the making of this story, rather it's been a listening ear, reading chapters, fleshing out ideas, choosing names, sending music that spoke to a specific character's personality, etc. This journey has been thrilling and I LOVED WRITING THIS PIECE so much so, that it turned into a three book series. My beta readers, Marva

(mommy … I heart you), Shanda, and Sharon, your feedback
is always welcomed and appreciated. My editor, MarZé Scott,
you did an amazing job!

Readers, I hope I did you proud and you enjoy this story.
You're who I do this for. Thanks for your continued support!
Until the next story …

One Love,

London St. Charles

Chapter 1

"How about a morning delight to get this twenty-fifth anniversary started off right," Jami whispered, sliding behind his wife, pulling her backside close to him. He draped a leg over Harper's hip, kissing her exposed shoulder that peeked from under the sheets. "I can give you a prelude to what I have in store for you this weekend."

"Slow down, Jami." Harper giggled, peeling his fingers from her waist. She rolled over and faced him as she readjusted the covers over her bare breasts. "I have something to tell you."

"That you love me and can't believe we've been married for a quarter of a century." Jami smiled, tracing Harper's pouty lips with his tongue. "Happy anniversary, honey."

"Happy anniversary," Harper replied, falling into the rhythm of Jami's passionate kiss. After a minute or so, she pulled away, clutching the comforter close to her chest. "Twenty-five years is a long time to love one person."

"Thirty, if you're counting from when we first started dating."

At the tender age of sixteen, Jamison Wilcox and Harper Moore fell in love. With the exception of student council meetings, dance, and fencing practice, they were inseparable. Like most high school sweethearts, they dreamed of getting married one day. Fortunately for them, they beat the odds and made a life out of what most adults considered puppy love.

"My entire adult life has been tied to you," Harper commented with a dull glance and a hint of sarcasm, tossing the covers back as she climbed out of bed.

Though Harper's statement was true, he didn't appreciate or deserve the tone in which it was given, but he overlooked it since she'd just woken up. Jami shifted onto Harper's pillow, inhaling the faint smell of cocoa butter and peaches while his awe-struck eyes focused on her irresistible figure, cross the length of the bedroom before disappearing into the bathroom across the hall.

The click of the door closing broke the spell. Jami blinked several times, adjusting himself. Harper's presence was enough to make his nature rise. She's had that power since they were teenagers doing things they had no business. He rolled over and pulled the nightstand drawer open. In an instant, a smile tugged the corners of his lips as he retrieved an envelope that contained two first-class airline tickets to Nashville, Tennessee.

The bathroom door creaked, causing Jami to jump to his feet. He tucked the tickets behind his back in the waistband of his camouflage boxers.

"I need to tell you something," Harper said, entering the bedroom, wearing a sheer white robe with red roses that left nothing to the imagination.

Jami reached for her hand, guiding Harper to the bed. They lowered in unison, angling their bodies toward one another.

An uncomfortable silence filled the space between them while Jami patiently waited for her to speak. Jami searched Harper's eyes, but she lowered her glance. He followed her gaze to their intertwined fingers that fit together like chocolate and vanilla swirl ice cream.

"Things between us haven't been the best," she finally said, running the tip of her thumb over her polished pink fingernails.

"They haven't been bad," Jami contested, searching Harper's solemn expression. "We have a good marriage."

"But things haven't been good either," Harper countered, lifting her eyes until they met Jami's. "If you're being honest with yourself, you would agree with me." She paused, swiping her waist-length box braids over her shoulder. "The first word that comes to mind when I think of our marriage is—— mundane."

It was Jami's turn to be quiet.

Harper worked part-time at the hospital as a mammography technician, and Jami as an over the road truck driver. He'd be gone for three weeks at a time with only two days off, so he was barely home. When Jami was home, spending time with his wife and two daughters was a top priority, but the only thing his body could do was shut down and sleep for twelve plus hours. Then, back on the road he went.

"I'll be the first to admit that things aren't as exciting as they used to be, but that doesn't mean we have a bad marriage," Jami said, scooting closer. "That's why this week is so important."

"Jami——"

"Shhhh." He placed his lips to hers, silencing Harper's speech. "I asked you to schedule this week off because I have something special planned for us. I know I've promised to take you places in the past, and something would always occur that prevented it from happening——mainly my job, but this time is different. You've been so patient with me and I appreciate that."

"You don't have to work like you do," Harper interjected. "I can pick up more hours if it means you'll be home more. I've told you that."

Jami sighed, resting a hand on Harper's thigh. "Let's not rehash this. Not today."

"Then when?" she asked, folding her hands in her lap. "If I blink my eyes, you'll disappear back to that trucking company."

"Don't do that," Jami recoiled, sliding a palm over the rumpled comforter, and grabbing a fist full of padded fabric. "Everything I do is for this family. You wanted to raise the girls on your terms, and I supported that. I never gave you push back for staying home with them. Not once. That meant I had to grind on a different level to carry the weight of a family of four, and that's what I did," he said, taking a deep breath, controlling the annoyed tone that threatened to surface. "Twenty-seven years later, I'm one of the highest-paid truckers with the company. That didn't happen by accident. I work hard so you don't have to. We have a good life. Don't try to make me feel bad for providing for our family."

"But Danica and Kylie are grown now," Harper replied, leaning forward. "I want your time. I don't need your money."

"Harvard law and orthodontist school say otherwise. All they see is green." Jami lightly chuckled, sliding a finger alongside Harper's face. "Babe, just hang in there a little while longer. We're over halfway to the finish line. Danica has one more year at Harvard. Once she graduates, I guarantee you, I'll be home more. I'm lonely too. I miss you more than you know."

"I can't wait another year," Harper said, sliding off the edge of the bed, walking toward the closet. "I want out. Now."

Jami straightened until both of his feet were firmly planted on the floor. He needed to feel rooted. His foundation cracked into a million pieces right before him. Absorbing the weight of Harper's words, Jami pushed himself upward. Before he could move, she exited the closet in a bright peach sundress and straw hat with a suitcase in tow.

"I'm going to Jamaica with my girls." Harper unzipped the outside compartment of her designer luggage, retrieving a tan file folder. She sighed, inching the princess-cut diamond wedding band from her left ring finger, then handed it to Jami. "You're a nice guy, I just don't want to be married to you anymore."

Chapter 2

Harper gripped the handle and tilted the suitcase on its wheels, taking long strides to exit the bedroom before Jami had a chance to say anything. She didn't want to hurt him. Harper loved Jami with everything she had, but that was no longer enough. She yearned to be free.

"What is this?" Jami questioned, anxiety lacing his tenor voice.

Pausing in the doorway, fighting back the tears, she replied, "Divorce papers."

Jami's silence spoke louder than a boxing ring announcer shouting, "Let's get ready to rumble."

Harper adjusted the straw hat, taking a step forward.

"Thirty years, two children, and our whole life together summed up in a legal document. Don't you think you owe me more than that?"

She sighed, turning to face her husband whose expression was one of hurt, shock, and confusion. Jami's wholesome orbs were pleading for an explanation.

"It's better this way."

"Better for who?" he asked, holding Harper's ring between his fingers, extending his arm forward. "Woman. Talk to me."

Harper clenched her teeth and swallowed as Jami rubbed a hand across his baldhead, shortening the distance between them.

"This isn't working for me anymore."

"Is there someone else?"

"Why does it always have to be another man involved when a woman wants to step away? I'm not cheating nor do I have any interest in doing so. I want to be free."

"What does that even mean——*free*?" Jami asked, twisting his full lips. "You need a change of scenery. Take a trip with your girls to blow off some steam, have fun, do crazy things that I'll never know about, and regroup, which apparently, you've already planned *on our anniversary*." Jami frowned, glaring at Harper with an intensity that weakened her resolve, but only for a moment. "You don't serve your husband divorce papers, *especially* not on your anniversary. What have I done so horrible to deserve such little regard?"

"This has nothing to do with you," Harper shouted,

immediately wishing she hadn't been so harsh. "I'm sorry for yelling. I——want. No, I *need* to experience life without you. I know that sounds awful, but that's how I feel."

"That's cruel and insensitive."

"I don't know what more you want me to say." She shrugged, turning her palms heavenward and pursing her lips.

"A real explanation wouldn't hurt," Jami replied, clutching the ring that once adorned Harper's hand in his. "I'm trying to understand, and I feel like you're toying with me."

Harper removed the straw hat, and tossed it onto the bed. "I feel like you've stayed with me this long out of obligation to my mom."

"You can't be serious right now." Jami's arms fell to his sides. "Yes, I promised your mother in her final days that I would take care of you, giving her peace of mind knowing that you would be cared for, making her transition easier. But wasn't that our plan all along——to get married after college? We both wanted that. You can't rewrite history to make it fit your current plan," Jami remarked, reaching for Harper's hand. "I'm with you because I want to be. I loved you then, and I still love you."

"Admit it. You aren't happy."

"Happiness is a state-of-mind, therefore I'm always happy," Jami said, pulling Harper so close to him that she could feel his breath sweep across the side of her face and neck. At one time, that nearness would've lit a fire in her nether regions.

"Taking care of you and the girls, makes me happy," he expressed, tilting her chin upward. "Knowing that my wife has no financial worries, makes me happy. Knowing my girls have completed their undergrad studies, and seizing the opportunity to thrive in their fields of specialty without worrying about how the tuition's going to get paid, makes me happy."

"You're talking about money," Harper commented, admiring Jami's smooth cocoa skin. "I'm talking about being fulfilled. Feeling alive and wanted. I don't feel like you desire me."

"That couldn't be further from the truth," Jami said in a low tone, releasing her hand. "You don't know me at all." He narrowed his gaze on her. "The weekly handwritten cards and flowers expressing my love for you. Your favorite lunch delivered to your job every Tuesday because that's the day the restaurant receives it's fresh seafood delivery. What about the reoccurring fifty dollars that I put on your Starbucks card every Sunday night because you always forget to reload it and I know how much you love your coffee?" Jami swallowed, shaking his head. Harper couldn't mistake the hurt in his eyes. "I have the neighbor pull the trash cans to the alley on pick-up day, mow the lawn and shovel the snow so you don't have to worry about it while I'm on the road."

"You have Mr. Summer's do that?" Harper asked not able to mask the surprise in her voice. "I thought he was just being a good neighbor."

"Of course I do. I care about your well-being. There's more to this than the fun stuff. If my everyday actions don't show it, in spite of me not physically being home, then I don't know. Maybe you really do have me pegged all wrong."

She pondered that for a minute. Harper didn't take into account all the little things that happened daily that made her life easier. *Am I being selfish?*

"Are you going to just ignore me?" Jami questioned with his hand extended, holding two envelopes.

Harper was so deep in her thoughts that she hadn't even noticed. She grabbed one of the blank white letter-sized envelopes and flipped it to the back, tugging at the sealed corner. "Are you serving me papers, too?" She snickered, slipping her thumb between the broken seal, inching it across to the opposite side. "Wouldn't that be something." Harper slid her lips to one side as she glanced at Jami, whose expression was tight. Placing her focus back on the what she was doing, Harper plucked a rectangular slip, and examined it. "First-class tickets to Nashville. Wow," she whispered, angling a glimpse at him. "You actually followed through on something. But, why Nashville? What's so special about Tennessee?"

"Please stop with the sarcasm. You're making it really hard for me to be decent." Jami swallowed so hard that it sounded like he gulped down a huge drink of water that got stuck in the back of his throat. "I've had about all the disrespect I'm going to take from you."

Harper huffed, slamming her hands on her hips, creasing the airline ticket. She didn't utter another word. Jami had never talked to her like that. He was upset. Instead, she focused on the crystal vase filled with aquamarine rocks on the bookshelf behind Jami.

Jami released a mournful sigh. "I've been working more

than usual so I could accumulate four weeks of paid leave to do something special for you. For us. We need time to reconnect." He gave Harper a half smile. "I know how much you love nature and hiking, so I rented us a cozy romantic cabin in the woods. It has a Jacuzzi, a pool table, an old school pinball machine, and a slew of board games."

Harper shifted her gaze to him.

"If I didn't want or desire you, then I wouldn't have gone through all of this to create the prefect getaway filled with the things you enjoy the most."

"I appreciate all that you've done for me, but it's too late now."

"Nothing is ever too late if we want the same thing. I'm mad as hell for what you did, but that doesn't mean I'm not willing to work on us."

"Jami, I'm sorry," Harper said, wiping the lone tear that had the nerve to run down her cheek. "I still need to explore life on my own."

"You mean without me," he whispered stepping backward.

"I don't know who I am outside of being Mrs. Jamison Wilcox," she admitted, retrieving the straw hat and placing it on her head. "I need to remember who Harper Moore was, and everything she aspired to be before I became a wife and mother."

"Wow. That's deep," Jami replied, pursing his lips. "You can step away from being my wife, but you can't ever stop being a mother to Danica and Kylie."

"I know that, *Jamison*," she fired back, walking toward the door, and gripping the handle of the suitcase. "I would never do that."

"First time in a while that you called me Jamison. I must've struck a nerve."

Harper gave him the nickname Jami when they were in high school, and that's how his friends and family have addressed him ever since.

"I have to go."

"So, you're really going to do this?" he asked, moving forward. "What about our trip?"

"You go. It doesn't make sense for you to lose all of the money because I'm not going."

"It's not even about the money," Jami expressed, reaching for her hand, but she pulled away. "I love you and I want our marriage to work," he pleaded. "Tell you what——come on the trip, and if you feel the same afterward, then I'll sign the papers."

The desperation in his voice did nothing for Harper. She had made up her mind.

"I'm keeping my plans with Bianca and Michelle. We're flying into Montego Bay this afternoon," Harper disclosed, not wanting Jami to think she was being sneaky. "I love you, but I have to be true to myself."

"What about the girls? What do we tell them?"

"Right now, nothing," she said, placing the envelope and ticket on top of the mocha cube organizer by the bedroom door. "They don't need to worry about our mess while they're in Miami. Let them enjoy the last days of their vacation. We'll talk to them when I get back." Harper turned on her heels, grabbed the suitcase handle, then said, "Bye," as she walked out of the bedroom.

She didn't look back, not even once.

Chapter 3

Jami stood stupefied, staring at the crumpled ticket. "Woooo." He waggled an index finger as if he were giving Harper a tongue lashing, which ended in him releasing a series of breathy chuckles and dragging the palms of his hands over his face. Hurt turned to anger, then controlled hysteria. He couldn't believe she discarded the ticket as if it were trash.

He hopped into a pair of striped lounge pants, slipped on black leather slides, then stepped out of the bedroom into the hall in just enough time to see Harper struggle, pulling another suitcase and duffle bag from the front closet.

"How long had she been packed?" he murmured under his breath. "This was her intention all along."

She glanced at him expectantly. "Can you help me?"

The nerve. "Nah, you want to experience life without me, remember? Well, here's your crash course," Jami remarked, folding his arms. "While you were planning your great escape, it seems like you forgot about the little things."

"Really, Jami?" She huffed, hiking the duffle bag straps on her shoulder. "Don't be that guy."

"Carry your own damn bags," he spat, going back into the bedroom.

Harper shouted several obscenities, forcing Jami to close the door to tune her out. He was still in shock. What type of guy did she expect him to be? Apparently, she didn't appreciate the considerate one.

He cracked the door and listened for a few minutes more as things bumped and crashed to the floor. He couldn't tell if she was carrying on to get his attention, or if she genuinely needed his help. Nevertheless, Jami's conscious wouldn't allow him not to aid Harper, regardless of his anger or how much she didn't deserve his kindness.

Exiting their bedroom, Jami maneuvered down the hall, entering the all-white decorated living room. It looked like a child had scribbled with a grey crayon along the foyer by the front door, probably from the suitcase scraping the wall.

"Is this everything?" he asked, removing the duffle bag from her shoulder, and lifting the large suitcase.

"Yes," Harper mumbled, her light maple-brown skin flushed pink. "The other bag is by the car."

Jami moved around her, stepping into the bright morning

sun. He placed the bags in the trunk and couldn't help but reflect on all the covert things Harper had done behind his back. Perhaps he was the one who didn't know his spouse.

He glared at the stranger who stood before him, trying to figure out when things went wrong.

"I'll be back next Friday. Eric has my spare key. He and EJ are coming by Wednesday to pick up a few of the things that I have packed in the garage to take to my apartment. I'll get the rest once I return."

"Your brother and nephew know what's going on? How many other people are in the loop besides me?"

"It's not even like that," Harper defended, opening the driver's side door. "I needed Eric's help. I had no choice but to tell him what was going on. He refused to assist me until I did. Believe me, I'm not out here parading around our problems to everyone."

"You're the only one who has a problem with things," Jami digressed, counting to ten in his head to keep from saying something he couldn't take back. "The girls will be home from their trip by the time we're supposed to return from Tennessee. I'm sure they'll notice your things missing."

"We'll talk to them."

"It's amazing to me how you keep saying *we'll* talk to Danica and Kylie, when *you're* the one who made a unilateral decision for the both of us," Jami snarled, waving her off. "You do whatever. I'll speak with my daughters on my own accord." He turned on his heels and headed up the walkway to the house. "Enjoy your trip."

Jami crossed the threshold and slammed the door before Harper had a chance to pull away from the curb. He glanced down at the scuff mark on the wall, stooped, then slid two fingers across the surface. Harper had chipped the paint.

He smirked, shook his head, then whispered, "More collateral damage."

Jami flinched at the sound of the landline ringing. No one called the house phone other than his parents when they couldn't get a hold of him on his cell phone. He clutched the sides of his pants. He did not have his phone with him. Jami rushed to the kitchen, checked the caller ID, and as predicted; Alice Wilcox's name flashed across the display in orange lights.

"Hey, momma."

"How did it go? Was she surprised?" Alice asked, excitement dripping from her voice.

He removed the phone from his ear, took a deep breath, then responded, "She loved it."

Jami didn't have the heart to tell his mother that Harper left him on their anniversary. He was embarrassed and ashamed and was doing his best to disguise his true feelings.

"I told you she would. Y'all be careful in them woods. This is bear season," Alice warned. "I don't want to hear about a black couple in the woods being eaten by a bear on the ten o'clock news."

"Momma, stop being overly dramatic."

"Tell me you haven't heard about a bear breaking into a cabin in the woods last week in Colorado, attacking a man."

"That's an isolated incident," Jami shot back.

"But it's not," Alice countered. "Days before that, a bear had descended on a family barbequing and stole a steak off the grill. Luckily, no one got hurt. Need I go on?"

"No ma'am," Jami surrendered with a chuckle. No way was he going to win this argument.

Truthfully, he wasn't even sure if he was still going. The cabin's a couple's getaway. How would it look with him showing up alone?

"Let me speak with Harper for a minute," Alice said. "I'll make sure she'll keep you in check. You know how you like to explore the unknown."

Jami shuddered. "She's in the shower."

"Is something wrong? You sound funny."

"I'm not sure what you mean," Jami covered, grabbing a bottle of water from the refrigerator. "I'm trying to get our things together so we can head to the airport."

"What time is your flight?"

"Twelve seventeen, but you know we need to be at the airport a couple of hours early to go through security."

"That's right," she replied. "Well, you make sure she calls me back."

"I will."

"And stay your behind out of them woods at night."

"Okay, momma."

"Jami, I mean it," she said with a bit more edge in her tone.

"I will. I promise."

"Have a safe flight and call me when you land. Happy anniversary."

"Thanks." He ended the connection, perching on the barstool.

Jami unscrewed the cap and downed about half the bottle of water before he took a breath. He could count on one hand the number of times he had lied to his mother. He hated to do it, but Jami wasn't ready for the interrogation that was sure to follow.

He finished the water and tossed the plastic bottle into the recycle bin, then headed down the hall to their bedroom. As soon as he crossed the threshold, Harper's lingering scent filled his nostrils. He always loved the alluring smell. Now, it was a reminder of the tornado that whipped through his marriage less than thirty minutes prior.

Glancing to the side, his eyes fell upon the airline ticket, sitting next to their twenty-year anniversary photo of them renewing their vows. He sighed, lifting the elegant gold garland frame. Harper looked like a queen from a long lineage of royalty in a sequin champagne evening gown and a stunning headpiece. Jami complimented her in a black tuxedo with a champagne paisley vest set, completed with matching necktie, cravat, pocket square, and cufflinks.

Emotions built up in Jami's chest, and it took everything in him not to shed a tear. He couldn't peel his eyes away from the magnificent photo, remembering what all it represented. Jami's eyes watered, making it impossible for him to hold back any longer. Luckily, the cell phone rang.

Perfect timing. He blinked away the tears, placed the photograph back on the shelf, then moved to the chest to retrieve his phone.

"Hey, Trevor. What's good?" he asked his best friend and fellow trucker of ten years.

"I wanted to catch you before you and Harp were all boo'd up in the lover's cabin, a happy anniversary. I can't believe she's put up with you this long," Trevor teased, laughing. "But seriously, twenty-five years is a blessing. Y'all give me and Bianca something to strive toward—— can you say marriage goals."

"Thanks," Jami responded, barely above a whisper."

"You don't sound like a man who's about to be knee deep in some lovin'. What's that about?" Trevor huffed, "I should be the one sad. My wife will be in Jamaica for the next seven days. I tried to get all the loving I could before dropping Bianca off at the airport."

Jami didn't say anything. He couldn't form the words.

"Hey, Jami. Are you there?"

"I'm here."

"Soooo, what's up?"

"We're not going," Jami confessed, moving to the window and peering out at the manicured lawn.

"Man, quit playing with me."

"I'm dead ass serious."

Trevor was so quiet on the other end that Jami swore the call dropped. He knew better though. The shock of the news messed Trevor up. How could it not? Jami was still stunned.

"Harper served me divorce papers this morning. She said needed to explore life without me, whatever the hell *that* means," Jami remarked, swiping the vertical blinds with such force that he knocked a couple of the panels loose.

"The fuck?" Trevor paused, and that weird silence permeated the air again. "I'm sorry, man."

"It's cool. I'm dealing——more like reeling, but I'll be all right," Jami said, stepping over the broken blinds, not caring that he destroyed them. "She's on the plane to Jamaica with Bianca and Michelle."

"What you saying, man?" Trevor's voice deepened. "Bianca knew about this?"

"I don't know who knew what."

"Well, let me assure you that I didn't know about any of it. I'd never keep anything like that from you," Trevor exclaimed, pleading his case. "You're my boy. You brought me and my wife together. I'd never condone, much less, be a part of such a betrayal."

Jami believed him. He'd be lying if he said it didn't cross his mind, thinking Bianca might have told Trevor in confidence.

"I'm going to cancel this trip. The airline won't refund my money, but they'll credit my account. As long as I fly within a year, I'm good.

"Man, go on that trip. You sacrificed a lot to make this happen. I know it's not the ideal circumstance, but you should still go. Let it be a sabbatical to clear your mind, relax, if that's even possible, and figure out your next move."

"You're right," Jami cosigned sounding more confident than he was. "I'm off the grid for the next seven days."

"There you go. If you need to talk, hit me up."

"Thanks, bro."

"You got it."

Chapter 4

Harper spotted Bianca's silky goddess locs, and Michelle's army buzz cut as she stepped off of the moving walkway at O'Hare International Airport. She smiled, approaching the boarding gate to Montego Bay, Jamaica. Her college roomies always brought joy to her spirit.

"Ladies," Harper crooned, standing behind her friends who sat with their heads bowed in perfect alignment with their phones.

"Oh my. I can't believe you're here," Michelle said, whipping her head to face Harper. "Does that mean …"

Bianca nudged Michelle, then maneuvered around the chairs and other passenger's luggage and hugged Harper. "You okay?"

"I'm good," Harper answered, arching her eyebrows and nodding.

Michelle joined them, and threw her short arms around Harper and Bianca's waist. "You sure? I didn't mean to be tactless."

"I've thought about this for a long time and I'm comfortable with my decision."

"But damn, Harp … on your anniversary?" Bianca scrunched her nose, giving Harper a side-eye. "That's deep, even for you."

"I don't want to get into all of that," Harper shot back, glancing from Bianca to Michelle, then back to Bianca. "I need this time to have fun with my *unjudgmental* friends."

"If you're cool, I'm cool." Bianca nodded.

"Me, too," Michelle added, touching the black, yellow, and green feather earring that matched her strapless wrap maxi dress. "Besides, we haven't been on somebody's island since graduation, and I'm ready to have some fun." Her eyes grew wide as she pointed at Harper. "Oh my gosh… remember, you got sick at the bubble pool party in Punta Cana?"

Harper laughed, hip bumping Michelle. "How can I forget."

"You threw up all over the place." Bianca chuckled, batting her eyelashes and shaking her head. "Them folks scattered out of that water faster than a roach when someone turned on the lights."

"You shut the party down, and not in a good way," Michelle added, bending over in gut-busting laughter.

"It ain't that damn funny," Harper remarked, stifling a chuckle of her own, glancing at the waiting travelers staring at them.

"You've always been able to hold your liquor," Bianca commented, as they reclaimed their seats with Harper sitting across from them. "I don't know what happened that day. You didn't even have that much to drink."

"I was eight weeks pregnant with Danica and didn't know it."

"That's right," Bianca replied, clasping her hands together.

"Funny how my major life changes surround our Caribbean trips … Danica, and now my divorce, twenty-seven years later."

"Don't look at it like that," Michelle said, waggling a finger. "Instead, embrace the fact that your besties have been with you during some of the most important times in your life."

"And we always will be," Bianca soothed, leaning forward, extending her arm in the aisle.

Harper and Michelle did the same, grabbing a hold of each other's hand, giving a reassuring squeeze.

"I love y'all so much," Harper said as the chorus of the song, *24K Magic* by Bruno Mars, played from her phone.

"You've got to be the only person on the planet that still has music ringtones," Michelle teased, leaning back in the seat.

"Shut up, Chelle," Harper chastised, sitting straight, and retrieving the phone from the side pocket of her purse. "That's my baby, Kylie."

Harper glanced at the picture that dawned on her phone of Kylie posing in the dentist chair, wearing a white lab coat and holding cleaning instruments. She was so proud of her youngest daughter's accomplishments. Kylie was twenty-four years old, and had completed her undergrad in three and a half years. She's in her third year of dental school, and after that, Kylie would be applying for a three-year residency program in advanced dentistry to become an orthodontist.

"See, you made me miss the call," Harper fussed, throwing a side-eye at Michelle.

The phone rang again, but this time, it was a FaceTime call from Kylie.

"Damn." Harper jumped out of her seat.

"What's wrong?" Bianca asked, coming forward, and so did Michelle.

Waving them back, Harper said, "Kylie's Facetiming me. She doesn't know about me and her dad. What am I going to do?"

"Answer it," Michelle replied, reaching over and tapping the green button on the screen.

"Whatcha go and do that for?" Bianca scolded through gritted teeth.

"It'll be weird if she doesn't answer her call," Michelle responded, tilting her head and smacking her lips.

"Hey baby." Harper smiled, shooing Bianca and Michelle away. "How's Miami?"

"It's great." Kylie beamed, showing off the whitest teeth

Harper's ever seen.

"You're a whole new shade of brown." Harper noticed, checking out Kylie's tan line on the halter bikini top.

"Yeah, more like toasted cinnamon, but I'll take it. These Miami men are loving all this melanin."

"Kylie Celeste Wilcox."

"Whoop," Michelle said, making pouty duck lips.

Bianca covered her mouth to stifle the laugh that seeped out.

Harper turned the phone faced down in her lap, and glared at her friends.

"Sounds like Harper 2.0 from our college days," Bianca whispered through her palm.

"Reincarnated," Michelle added, crossing her leg.

"Shut up," Harper mouthed, rolling her eyes.

"Mom."

"I'm here," she responded, flipping the phone over, surprised to see Danica on the screen with Kylie.

"We said happy anniversary," Danica repeated, looking refreshed, wearing orange lip gloss, with her hair gathered in a neat bun, and a suntan matching her sister's.

"Thank you," Harper replied, gazing at her beautiful daughters. "Danica… you keep an eye on Kylie. I can't have–
—"

"Mom, no worries," Kylie butted in, smoothing her dark-auburn bob that lined evenly against her jaw-line. "No one and nothing will distract me from finishing my dental program. Trust me on that."

"Ooooookay."

Harper knew she didn't have anything to worry about when it came to those two. There was no one more focused on their careers than her girls, but it still had to be said.

"Where's dad?" Kylie asked.

"We want to wish him happy anniversary, too before you lovebirds disappear into the woods. Dad gave us strict instructions not to call unless our lives were in grave danger, and he was the only person who could help us," Danica added, and Kylie giggled in the background.

"He's in the men's room."

Good afternoon passengers. This is the pre-boarding announcement for flight 615B to Montego Bay, Jamaica. Passengers with small children, and any——"

Harper pulled the phone close to her chest, and cupped a hand over the speaker. She walked toward the aisle while Bianca and Michelle grabbed their belongings.

"I thought y'all were going to Tennessee?" Danica said with a questioning pitch, proof that she overheard the boarding announcement. "Mom. Are you there?"

Harper remained silent, trying to collect her thoughts.

"Didn't dad tell us he was taking mom to Sevierville, Tennessee to some cabin?" Harper overheard Danica ask Kylie.

"That's what he said," she confirmed. "Mom, what are you doing?"

Harper glanced over at her friends who gazed at her in utter confusion. They couldn't help. She wasn't even supposed to be with them.

"I'm here."

Danica narrowed her wide-set eyes. "Are you and dad going to Jamaica?"

"No. We're only sitting in this area because no seats were available at our boarding gate, but Jamaica would be nice."

"Don't let dad hear you say that," Kylie cautioned, taking Harper by surprise. "He's been putting this together for a long time."

"I know, baby."

Kylie was always the one to come to Jami's defense. Harper didn't know why she was so shocked to learn that the girls knew more about the vacation than she did. They were daddy's girls, and Jami shared everything with them. But it was nice to know that Jami really did put effort into the trip. *The time she stopped believing in him.*

"I need to check on your dad. He's been in there too long," Harper said, glancing over at Bianca and Michelle who stared back at her with expectancy. "I'll tell your dad you called."

"Have a safe trip," Danica said with a wide grin. "And have fun."

"We love you," Kylie sang, blowing Harper a kiss.

Attention passengers, regular boarding for flight 615B will begin in five minutes. Please have your boarding pass and identification ready.

"I love you, too, and you girls enjoy your last three days in Miami, and let me know when you make it home."

"Harp," Michelle whispered, standing in front of her, tapping her watch.

"We will," Danica promised. "Bye, mom." They waved in unison.

Harper blew them a kiss, ending the call.

She slid the phone in the side pocket of her purse as Michelle reached for her hand. Harper allowed Michelle to guide her through the crowd like a wayward child being reprimanded, to where Bianca was standing, holding their place in line.

What have I done? Explaining things to my girls is going to be much harder than I thought.

Chapter 5

"Has anyone ever told you that you look like Morris Chestnut?" a woman of forty-plus years asked Jami, halting the traffic in the aisle as passengers tried to debark the plane in Nashville.

"He's my cousin," Jami replied with a straight face.

"Really," the ivory-skinned woman shrieked, turning beet red. "Can I take your picture?"

"Lady, come on," a man complained from a few rows back. "We don't have all day."

"Real quick," she said, leaning over, her breasts brushing

Jami's shoulder as she snapped a selfie. "Thank you so much. My friends aren't going to believe this."

"You're welcome," he replied, retrieving a bag from under the seat in front of him.

The man sitting in the same row as Jami by the window seat asked, "Are you really Morris Chestnut's cousin?"

"Nah." Jami grinned so hard his jawbone ached.

They shared a laugh and a fist bump.

Jami needed that comic relief. Anything to take his mind off of Harper was welcomed. He retrieved his luggage, got the keys for the all-terrain SUV rental, then hit the highway to Sevierville, Tennessee, which was a little over three hours away with no stops.

He cued the iTunes library in his phone to the infamous 2Pac playlist, and before he knew it, Jami was only fifteen minutes away from his destination. The jagged peaks of the Great Smoky Mountains reached into the clouds of the azure blue sky as he drove along the two-lane highway of hilly roads through acres of woods. Though he wasn't a country man, he enjoyed the peaceful scenery.

Harper would've loved this.

Jami turned off the highway onto a dirt and gravel road. Tall trees hovered over the vehicle until he reached a small body of water. Jami slowed, lowering the window, but quickly closed it as the pungent fishy smell made him choke. He winced, damn near rubbing his nose off of his face.

He followed the directions, leading him to cabin nine. Right below each sign was a reminder to not feed the bears and to make sure all trash is discarded in the bear-proof receptacle.

"Ohhhh, momma." Jami chuckled, reflecting on their earlier conversation.

Alice didn't have to worry. If the locals were warning tourists to be cautious of bears, then Jami would listen. He took a photo of the signage so he could show her when he returned to Chicago.

He pulled into the space in front of cabin nine, surprised to see another vehicle there. Stepping out of the SUV, Jami surveyed the area. A multitude of tress encompassed the cabin, making it invisible to passersby, unless they knew where they were going.

Jami felt eyes on him, coming from the woody area. He gradually turned his head to the right, peering into the thick brush. Though partially camouflaged, Jami exchanged glances with a female deer before she galloped deeper into the woods. He hadn't seen a deer that close before. She was beautiful. Jami took a baby step forward to see if there were any more deer nearby.

"I wouldn't do that," a firm, but sweet feminine voice said from behind. "It's a long way down from up here."

Jami slid his foot back, then turned to see who was speaking to him. The beauty resembled a modern day African American Pocahontas, but with red hair.

"The land looks flat due to the overgrown foliage, but don't let it fool you. The drop off is steep, trust me."

"I'll take you at your word," Jami replied, glancing over his shoulder into the woods, realizing that the deer wasn't eye level with him.

"Where's the misses?"

"Excuse me?" Jami's eyebrows shot up to his nonexistent hairline.

"I'm Aurora Delaney, the cabin owner," she greeted, tugging the fingertips of a work glove until it had been removed from her right hand, then extended her arm toward Jami. "We spoke on the phone a couple of times over the past few weeks."

"Yes. Of course." He reciprocated the gesture, noticing the softness of her hand. "Nice to meet you. Jamison Wilcox, but everyone calls me Jami."

"I like Jamison," she said, smiling. "It sounds distinguished."

"That's the first time I've been told that," he remarked, thinking of his name in a different light. "Um——." He scratched his head. "I'm surprised to see you. I thought it was keyless entry."

"It is. The keypad is mounted above the doorknob," Aurora clarified, shifting her weight, pointing toward the cabin. "The cleaning crew left about an hour ago. I like to go over the final details to make sure everything is up to par for my guests."

"I appreciate that personal touch as I'm sure all of your visitors do."

The corners of her lips curved upward as she glanced over at the empty SUV. "I also added the special items you requested. The champagne's on ice and the cake is in the refrigerator. I didn't want the balloons to deflate, so I had them delivered about fifteen minutes ago," she explained, plucking the left glove off of her hand and tucking them in her back pocket. "You're very thoughtful. I hope your wife knows how lucky she is."

"Thank you," Jami said, trying to hide the disappointment in his face and tone.

"I expected to be gone by the time you arrived. You're a bit early."

"My flight landed twenty minutes ahead of schedule, and the drive here from Nashville was uneventful, hardly any traffic. Besides, I wanted to get a lay of the land before heading to the city to buy groceries."

"Makes sense," she agreed, peeking over at the SUV a second time. "Is Mrs. Wilcox coming later?"

Jami shuffled the gravel with the tip of his shoes, sliding his hands into the pockets of his denim cargo shorts, feeling small for having to admit his truth. "I'm afraid she won't be joining me."

Aurora's eyes lowered to the rocky covered ground.

"I hope it's not a problem that I'm here alone. I know you cater to couples. I don't want to make anyone uncomfortable," he said, continuing to sift the gravel with his shoe. "I didn't find out she wasn't coming until this morning."

"It's okay," Aurora comforted, moving forward, touching his arm. "It's apparent from the extensive preparations that you booked the cabin with all intentions of her being here. It's very sweet. Most couples don't ask for these types of accommodations."

"Thanks for understanding," Jami said, lifting his arm to

check the time on his watch. "I'll be back in an hour or so. By then, I'll be able to check in and get settled."

"That's not necessary," Aurora insisted, applying gentle pressure to his arm. "The cabin's ready. I was arranging the decorations when you pulled into the driveway …" She glanced up at Jami, pausing for a moment. "I can remove them if you want."

"Your kindness is noted, but I'll take care of it. You've been more than helpful."

***

A knock on the door startled Jami, causing him to scramble to a sitting position. He'd fallen asleep on the sectional with the car keyring still looped around his middle finger.

"Jamison, it's Aurora," she called out with a series of hard knocks. "Are you, all right?"

Dropping the keys on the sofa, he drew both hands to his face, rubbed his eyes, then opened them for the first time. The room was dark. Not pitch black, but dim from the shadow casted over the cabin from the trees hovering above, blocking majority of the sunlight. The fact that no lights were on didn't help.

"Your trunk's open."

Adrenaline slammed into his pulse, making Jami fully aware. He fetched the keys, then stepped over the wooden coffee table, instead of maneuvering the obstacle course that his suitcases created on both sides of him.

Swinging the door open, he stopped in his tracks. Stacked food storage containers, a pair of arms barely holding them, and Aurora's face from the nose up, greeted him. Familiar soul food aromas wafted in the country air, reminding Jami of Sunday evenings at his grandparent's house as a child.

"I hope I'm not overstepping. I thought you could use a homecooked meal. My mother's soul food always made my father feel better after a rough day."

Jami slipped a hand underneath the storage containers, brushing Aurora's arm. Her mocha skin felt soft as a rose petal dipped in oil. "Thank you. You didn't have to do this, but I'm glad you did." He inhaled the southern goodness. "I haven't eaten since last night's dinner. As you may have guessed, I haven't been to the store as planned." He glanced beyond Aurora's beautiful head of wavy scarlet hair to his truck.

"Don't worry, everything's in place. One of the workers spotted your trunk open and told me. I'm across the way in cabin eight," she informed, pointing to the right. "I closed it once I realized you hadn't come back out after a while."

"That sofa beckoned to me, and the next thing I know, you're knocking on the door."

"I know what you mean. I have the same one in my cabin and it *is* rather comfortable." Aurora giggled, sweeping the long tresses over her left shoulder. "I didn't want to bother you. I contemplated leaving the food at the door with a note, but it might attract the bears."

The voice of Jami's mother popped into his head.

"That must've been some nap," Aurora teased.

"What time is it?" Jami asked, listening to the different insects hum, buzz, and chirp nearby, a stark contrast from the sounds he's used to hearing in the city.

"About eight fifteen or a little after."

A moist wind passed through the air, creating an even muggier feel.

"I'm not going to take up anymore of your time," Aurora commented, stepping backward onto the gravel driveway. "I hope you enjoy your dinner. Have a good night."

"Wait a minute." Jami crossed the threshold, moving in her direction. "There's no way I'm going to let you prepare a meal, and not partake in it. Please, have dinner with me."

"I don't want to impose on your time."

"Too late." He winked, then nodded toward the front door. "Join me."

Chapter 6

"Relax. I'll make our plates." Jami moved around the log cabin style kitchen, checking the wooden cabinets and drawers for dinnerware, and serving spoons.

"Let me help," Aurora insisted, joining Jami in the kitchen. "I know where everything is."

"No, I have it," Jami countered, pulling white plates with sunflower designs on the rim, and matching mugs from the cabinet above the sink. "It's the least I can do for the person who prepared the meal."

He found the silverware and serving spoons, washed, and rinsed everything, then dried them with a paper towel.

"You know your way around a kitchen," Aurora

complimented, taking a seat on the round wooden barstool. "I'm impressed."

"Don't assume because I'm a man that I don't have any domestic skills," Jami boasted as he set a dish in front of Aurora.

"That's not what I'm saying," she explained, placing her elbows on the table, resting her pointy chin in her hands. "I mean, for you not to be familiar with this setup, you're working it like you've been here before."

"Nice save." Jami chuckled, unpacking the three large storage bowls, filled with collard greens, macaroni, fried chicken, and cornbread muffins. He spooned healthy amounts of each southern delicacy onto Aurora's plate, then grabbed a moist muffin.

Aurora pushed her hand forward, almost knocking the cornbread to the floor. "No, thank you. Bread and I have an emotionally abusive relationship."

"You're hilarious. It's cornbread," he teased, maneuvering the golden-crowned muffin around her hand. "What are you going to use to sop up the juice from the greens?"

"Not that."

Jami removed the moist goodness from her plate, and placed it on a saucer. "I'll leave it there in case you change your mind."

He claimed the seat across from Aurora, which faced the all-season sunroom and piled his plate with all of the fixings Aurora provided. Jami inhaled a deep, quiet breath as his eyes drew upward to the raised wooden center beam that created a cathedral ceiling effect. The balloons, champagne on ice, two flutes, chocolate covered strawberries, his and hers bath robes, and battery-operated tea-light candles were on full display through the floor to ceiling glass panels. He couldn't shake his thoughts of Harper and the hurt she caused.

After a few moments of deafening silence, Aurora asked, "Do you want to talk about it?"

"No." He stabbed the collard greens with the fork, inserting several leafy pieces into his mouth. "Mmmm, this is delicious." He took another forkful, then placed the utensil on the edge of his plate. Covering his mouth while he chewed, Jami excused himself.

He dabbed the corners of his lips, then walked through the living room, passing the regulation sized pool table, and Jacuzzi before entering the sunroom. Gazing out of the sliding glass door, Jami stood awe struck by the array of red, orange, and yellow tints that casted shadows through the trees as the sunset in the woods. The online photos of the sun setting from previous guests were beautiful, but it looked even better in person. He retrieved the chilled wine from the bucket of half-melted ice and the champagne flutes, then returned to the kitchen.

"We might as well enjoy this. No need for perfectly good wine to go to waste." He twisted the cap until it cracked opened. Out of habit, Jami passed the rim of the bottle under his nose and inhaled the sweet, citrus flavors of oranges, green apples, strawberries, pineapples, and lemons. "Have some?"

"Don't mind if I do." Aurora held onto the stem and lifted the flute as Jami poured, filling her glass halfway. "I love sangria."

My wife does, too.

Several hours and two bottles of wine later, Jami's tongue was loose enough for him to speak candidly about Harper without falling apart. Aurora was the ear Jami didn't know he needed. She listened, and her compassionate expression made him even more comfortable.

"I'm sorry this happened to you. No one deserves to be treated so carelessly. Sounds to me like Harper's the one missing out," she remarked, slipping off the wedged sandals, and tucking her feet underneath her bottom as she leaned back into the sofa cushion. "It's unfortunate that she didn't come to you with her concerns. Unless you're putting on an act, you appear to be reasonable and level-headed, and I've only known you for a few hours."

Jami smiled at her banter, laying his head on the back of the sofa as he gazed into her engaging brown eyes.

"From everything you've told me, it seems like she has plenty of time to explore her interests. Many women would be blessed to have a husband like you."

"I have my faults, too. Harper claims I'm a workaholic and don't spend enough time with her." He paused, rubbing his chin. "Maybe she's right. Years of being on the road for months at a time would put a strain on anyone's marriage."

"Let me ask you something," Aurora said, placing a hand on Jami's knee. "Are you out there having fun, hanging in bars, picking up women?"

"I would never——No matter how lonely I've been——I

respect the sanctity of my marriage too much to do something vile."

Aurora gazed at him with pursed lips, tilting her head as if Jami had said something incredible.

"What? Why are you looking at me like that?"

"You're doing what women tend to do when their husband or boyfriend cheats or behaves the wrong way——they blame themselves. You've done nothing wrong."

"But I do work a lot."

"And so does the rest of society who want more for themselves and their family," Aurora shot back. "You're doing what you're supposed to do."

"What makes you the expert?"

"Because I'm a divorcée from a husband who complained of the same thing. The only difference is, my ex-husband was a cheat and had zero ambition. He thought it was okay to live off of the success that I built. He had no interest in my company at the grassroot stages when I begged him to go into business together."

"Sorry."

"No need to be. Hunter's disloyalty was the best thing that ever happened to me," she admitted, reaching for the flute and swallowing the last contents of the wine. "He had the nerve to have his mistress book one of my cabins, so they could spend the weekend together. The balls on this guy were beyond huge."

Jami was speechless. He would've never guessed the beautiful woman before him had been treated so poorly.

"You're not that guy," Aurora said, gesturing toward the

sunroom. "Look at what you've done to make this week special for your wife. You told me in your email that you didn't care for the woods——that it was too many bugs for you, but Harper loved nature, and you wanted to make this a vacation that she would never forget. Most men wouldn't do that. You put her wants before yours. That's the epitome of a loving and caring husband which is supposed to equate to a healthy marriage."

"When you put it like that, I don't feel as defeated." He placed a hand on top of Aurora's, that was still resting on his knee. "Thank you."

Aurora laid her free hand on top of his like they were in a huddle with a coach before a big game. She moved in closer, placing her head on the back of the sofa, giving Jami direct eye contact. "You're welcome."

They sat in silence for several minutes. The worries of the past eighteen hours had dissipated, and the wine had taken full effect, creating the perfect uber-relaxed state.

***

A howling wind, and rattling sounds brought Jami back to life. He opened his eyes, instantly feeling pressure on his chest. Glancing down, Aurora's candy apple red hair greeted him. He had no idea how long they've been sleep, but it had to be in the wee hours of the morning.

Jami tried to ease from underneath Aurora, lowering her head to the cushion without waking her, but as soon as he moved, she wrapped an arm around his waist as if holding a pillow. Her head now resting in his lap.

He found solace in Aurora's hold on him. It reminded Jami of the times when Harper snuggled close to him after they'd finish making love. Intimacy was something he craved more than anything.

Jami adjusted, trying to get comfortable, but Aurora wasn't letting him go, so he tolerated the awkward position until his leg and foot went numb.

"Aurora. Aurora," he called out, sweeping the hair from her angelic face. "Aurora."

She stirred, releasing the grasp as she stretched her arms.

"Heyyyyy," Jami crooned, rotating his foot in a circle. "Wake up sleeping beauty."

"Oh my," Aurora pushed back until she was upright. "What time is it?"

"Déjà vu," he teased, standing to get the blood circulating while enduring the pins and needles that raced up and down his leg.

"What?"

He chuckled, realizing she didn't get the joke. Jami limped to the kitchen to grab his phone from the table. "It's three-thirty-five."

She stood, smoothing her hair and clothes. "I have to go. I didn't mean——"

"It's all right. Neither one of us planned for the evening to go this way, but I'm glad it did," Jami admitted, coming back into the living room, walking with a normal gait. "I enjoyed your company."

Aurora slipped on her sandals, and headed for the door. "Wash the containers when they're empty and leave them on the counter. I'll collect them at the end of the week. Have a goodnight."

"Hold on," Jami said, pulling on his sneakers. "I'll walk you to your cabin."

"It's just across the way."

"And I'm still going to make sure you get there safely. It's pitch black."

"I can navigate these woods blindfolded."

"That may be true, but I'm still walking you home." Jami maneuvered around the coffee table and joined Aurora by the door.

Aurora went into the kitchen and retrieved a flashlight from under the sink. "You're going to need this."

Jami opened the door, pressed the black button, and the light illuminated the darkness. "After you."

Their feet crunched over the gravel as they trekked across the road. The insects let their presence be known with every sound they made, guiding them along the way. Within eight minutes, they were on Aurora's doorstep.

Jami held her hand as she climbed the stairs.

"Satisfied," she teased, pressing the code into the keypad.

"Yes, I am."

"Goodnight, Jamison," Aurora brushed his cheek with the palm of her hand. "Thanks for being a gentleman."

Chapter 7

Damn, he's fine. Harper slid on her shades to get a better look at the handsome brown-skinned specimen coming their way, without being too obvious. Something about openly appreciating a man other than her husband was foreign.

"Welcome to Jamaica, ladies," he greeted with a heavy island accent, blinding them with his gleaming smile as he entered the main lobby of the cabana.

"Why, thank you." Michelle spun slowly on her heels, checking out his firm backside with no shame. "Lawd, have mercy. I need me some of that this week."

"How old are you?" Bianca chuckled, lifting a medium-arched brow.

"Forty-four, single, and ready to mingle with the natives," Michelle raised a hand, giving Harper a high-five. "What's your point?"

"And you're cosigning?" Bianca gave Harper a side-eye.

"Heyyyy, I'm just here for the ride," Harper said, splaying her fingers in front of her.

"You should get a taste too with your newfound freedom," Michelle encouraged, hip bumping Harper, as they stepped outside into the pool-bar area. "Thirty years of the same package has got to be boring."

Harper could think of numerous words to describe she and Jami's bedtime rendezvous, but boring wasn't one of them. The sex was mind-blowing—*when she got it*. That was the real problem. Jami's schedule left little room for them to enjoy one another or do anything else.

They settled pool-side in the chaise lounge patio chairs with the cushy built-in foam headrests. Harper lifted her shades, resting them at her hairline so she could take in the clear blue skies, and even clearer crystal water. The palm trees demanded attention as they swayed in the warm gentle breeze.

"Good day. I'm Chilton. May I get you ladies something to drink?" the cabana attendant asked, dressed in all white linen pants and a button-down.

Bianca and Michelle ordered mojitos, and Harper a piña colada.

"Coming right up," he said, rushing off to the bar.

"Even the staff is fine," Michelle commented, following the attendant with her eyes until he was out of sight.

Harper stood in agreement. The eye candy was definitely appealing.

Within ten minutes, Chilton returned with their drinks on a serving tray. "This is from the gentleman at the bar." He handed Harper two folded napkins.

She followed the direction Chilton nodded in, making eye contact with the gorgeous man with locs, braided in a mohawk style with shaved sides, and a full, trimmed beard.

"Enjoy."

The man smiled at Harper, then raised his drink in a congratulatory way. Goosebumps pricked her skin, and a chill coursed through her body that didn't match the current climate.

"Open it, Harp," Bianca pushed, her anxiousness on full display.

"Come on, already," Michelle added, leaning forward, damn near in Harper's lap.

Drinks on me, beautiful one. Enjoy your day. Please join me for dinner this evening. Let's meet at the gazebo at seven. I'll be waiting. DaJuan.

Harper folded the napkins, placed them on the patio table, and sat the corner of her cocktail glass on the end of it to keep them from blowing away.

"So, what are you going to do?" Bianca asked, glancing over at DaJuan who stared in their direction. "He hasn't taken his eyes off of you yet."

"I don't know," she replied, glancing across the pool area

to the far side of the resort where the gazebo sat on a rock peninsula. "I bet that's real pretty at night," she mumbled.

"So, that means you're going, right?" Michelle asked.

"I don't know this man." Harper glanced over her shoulder at DaJuan. She frowned, but his charm disarmed her, but only for a second. "I don't care how good-looking he is. Hell, I'm not trying to be another statistic," she said making air quotes. "American woman goes missing in Montego Bay."

"What if we come too——to the pool area——right here," Bianca suggested, looking across the crowded space. "We have an unrestricted view of the gazebo."

"And our safety plan stays the same as our college days. No one leaves the resort without the other. No one goes anywhere without everyone knowing. When not together, we check in every thirty minutes." Michelle tilted her head down as if looking over a pair of glasses. "We got you. Go have fun."

Al Jarreau's song, *So Good*, pierced the air.

"You and these damn ringtones," Michelle snickered, shaking her head.

"That's Jami," Harper smirked, her finger hovering over the answer button. "Why's he calling me?"

Bianca shrugged.

"He needs a different ringtone if you insist on using them," Michelle teased, throwing her locs over her shoulder.

"Maybe it's a sign that I shouldn't do this."

"That's your conscious playing tricks on you," Michelle replied, touching Harper's arm. "You're not doing anything wrong, so stop putting yourself on a guilt trip."

"What if it's about the girls?"

"There's only one way to know," Bianca said, crossing her legs at the ankles. "Answer it."

The phone stopped ringing and the voicemail alert chimed.

Harper took a deep breath, pressing the blue speaker icon so everyone could hear, then the arrow for playback.

Hey. I was checking to see if you made it safely. I guess you're fine. Bye.

Even in disappointment and hurt, Jami was still looking out for Harper's well-being.

"That's a good brother there," Bianca commented.

Harper turned and glared at her. "Weren't you just encouraging me to go out with DaJuan?"

"That has nothing to do with Jami. He *is* a good dude. Always has been, but I'm not married to him," Bianca expressed, swirling the lime and mint leaves with the skinny black straw before taking a sip. "Only the two of you know what goes on in your marriage. I'm only speaking on what I've seen over the past twenty plus years."

"Don't do that to her," Michelle fussed, putting her focus on Bianca. "Harp made a decision based on what's best for her. Don't make her feel bad about it."

"I'm not," Bianca defended, placing the glass on the table. "I'm just saying, she could do a lot worse. Jami is one of the good ones——and he's fine as hell too, with that creamy chocolate skin, goatee, panty-dropping smile, and juicy lips like LL Cool J."

"Well, damn, Bianca," Michelle balked, flipping her locs.

"Do *you* wanna screw her husband?"

"Not at all. I'm just repeating the way Harper has described Jami on numerous occasions," Bianca shot back, mirroring Michelle's expression. "Don't act like you don't know. A blind chick could see how fine he is." Bianca chuckled. "You see Harper's not disagreeing with me, cause she knows her husband's that dude."

***

Harper gazed at herself in the full-length mirror, checking her profile from all angles. She wore an ocean blue Polynesian halter dress with a lace racer back, that accentuated her hour-glass curves. She lifted the dress and wiggled her all-white pedicured toes in the strappy silver sandals.

"Up or down?" she asked Bianca and Michelle, fiddling with her braids.

"You have a beautiful neck, so I say up," Bianca replied.

"I agree," Michelle chimed in, drawing a chair over, and placing it behind Harper. "Besides, you don't want your hair to take away from your dress design."

Harper claimed the seat while Michelle pulled her hair in a high ponytail, then wrapped it into an attractive bun.

"Now, you're ready," Michelle commented, grabbing Harper's silver clutch, and handing it to her.

"I'm going to call you at eight-thirty," Bianca said, setting the alarm on her phone. "An hour and a half is more than enough time to have dinner and small talk."

"Agreed," Harper replied, turning to face them. "If he turns out to be a bum, this gives me an excuse to leave."

Bianca nodded.

Harper took one last look in the mirror. "Let's do this before I lose my nerve."

Chapter 8

Harper took a deep breath, strolling along the pier to the gazebo that glistened with white Christmas lights, complimenting the peach and orange hues as the sun descended from the sky. The ocean twinkled and glimmered, creating one of the most breathtaking backdrops Harper's ever seen.

"Good evening," DaJuan greeted with an accent not quite as heavy as the man who spoke to them in the cabana. He looked even better than earlier, wearing a pair of cream skinny-fit chinos, a coral striped fitted polo, and dark-brown Ferragamo loafers. "I didn't know if you would come."

"I wasn't sure either," Harper's voice cracked from nervousness, taking in the white tulle looped around the inner post, and the small square table set for two. "When you asked me to join you for dinner, I didn't picture this."

A smile split his macchiato lips, which were the identical shade of the rest of his smooth skin.

"There are several gazebos on the island, however, this one is the best place to watch the sunset. I thought you'd like it."

If DaJuan did all of this to impress a woman on their first meeting, she could only imagine what he did on date number two. Although, this doesn't classify as a date.

"I do." Harper paused, hypnotized by the beautiful Caribbean Sea. "I love nature in its natural state, if that makes sense."

"It does. I sometimes fail to appreciate what's yahso every day, yuh kno?"

Harper's reply was delayed. She racked her brain, trying to remember the Jamaican Patois words and phrases that she studied in the translator book she purchased six months ago. She had been doing pretty good, until now. *Yahso, yahso——* she snapped her fingers, *right here.*

"Same thing happens back home," Harper said, proud that she understood DaJuan's vernacular. "I live in one of the most amazing cities, with astounding architecture, landmarks, and a lakefront like no other, but the people focus on the negative aspects of the city. I'm sometimes guilty of it too."

"Wah brings yuh an yuh friends tuh Jamaica?"

Harper leaned on the railing, and smiled at him. "I was wondering when I would hear your true native tongue. No disrespect. I mean, your English is superb."

"I sometimes slip into my laidback speech, but with my job, proper English makes it easier for folks to understand me," DaJuan explained, "but get me around my Jamaican brothers and sisters, an yuh wi speak fluent patwah by di end of di night."

"Look at you." Harper loved the way he was able to turn it on and off.

"You still haven't answered my question." DaJuan's heated gaze made Harper even more nervous than before. "What brings you here?"

"A much-needed vacation to relax with my girls," she declared, shifting her gaze in the direction of Bianca and Michelle.

DaJuan moved next to her, brushing his pinky finger across her left hand. "Where's your husband?"

Harper shifted her stance, creating an arm's length distance between them.

"I didn't mean to offend you," DaJuan explained, facing Harper and placing a hand over his heart. "I noticed the tan line on your left ring finger."

She glanced down, and the pale area where her wedding ring used to be, stood out even in the dim lighting.

"It's complicated." Harper didn't want to tell him any of her business. She didn't know him well enough.

"I understand." DaJuan ambled to a nearby table and pulled out the chair. "I have a complicated situation too."

Her eyes lowered to the masculine hands on the back of the chair before claiming the seat. She didn't see a wedding ring or a shadow indicating that something was once there. As much as Harper wanted to ask what his comment meant, she respected the reciprocity.

"Thank you." Harper smiled as he pushed up her seat.

"I ordered you a piña colada. I hope that wasn't presumptuous."

"Maybe a little, but that's fine," Harper teased, spotting the server coming down the pier in black slacks, a white shirt, bowtie, and suspenders.

"I like a funny woman." DaJuan grinned, throwing Harper a flirty side glance.

Harper's insides melted the way they used to when Jami paid her special attention; in the early days before work consumed his life. DaJuan made her giddy. No question that she was an attractive woman, but there was something about a good-looking man going out of his way to cater to her. Harper still had that thing that made men swoon, and if she ever doubted it, DaJuan's presence was all the validation she needed.

After dinner, they strolled along the pier, stopping short of the white sand beach. Harper bent to take off her sandals, but DaJuan knelt and did the honors. She lifted her dress mid-calf, giving him plenty of room to unbuckle the silver straps wrapped around her petite ankles.

DaJuan carried her shoes as they sauntered through the cool sand, ending at the shore line. She pinched the fine particles between her toes, inching forward until the warm rolling waves washed over her feet.

"You wanna sit?" DaJuan asked.

Harper glanced around. No lawn chairs were nearby. "I would love too, but I don't want to ruin my dress."

DaJuan took a knee. "You may sit here," he said, glancing up at Harper with a side grin, patting his knee. "I promise no funny business."

"Your pants——the salt water will ruin them." Harper gestured for DaJuan to rise.

"Ya mon." He reached for her hand, touching the tips of her fingers.

Harper's breath quickened with the slight, but tender touch. She lifted her dress to her knees, then lowered onto his thigh. The ocean breeze swirled around them, enhancing his natural masculine scent. He placed a hand on the small of her back, sending Harper's hormones into overdrive.

"Did you know the beaches here are man-made?"

"No——no, I didn't," she responded, keeping her gaze toward the ocean, willing the feelings she enjoyed coursing through her body to cease. Harper had never felt anything carnal for any man other than Jami.

"The resorts are built on areas where there is no beach. Negril has the best beaches in Jamaica. Maybe I can take you there before you leave."

"Maybe… "

And on cue, *What About Your Friends* ringtone, sang from her purse.

"Excuse me." Harper stood, retrieving the phone, then

moving a short distance away. Placing the phone to her ear, Harper whispered, "Girl thank you for stopping me from doing something stupid."

"You good?" Bianca asked.

"I am, now." She glanced over her shoulder at DaJuan, who was gazing at her with lustful eyes that made Harper's heart gallop. "I'll be right there. I can't trust myself alone with this man."

Chapter 9

"This had better be an emergency," Jami answered the phone, teasing Danica while hoisting an oversized backpack onto his shoulders. Even though the circumstances between him and Harper had changed, from when he gave that directive, the girls didn't know that.

"There's a tropical storm heading for Miami. The predicted landfall is within ten to twelve hours."

The backpack slithered down his arm, landing on the porch with a loud thud. "Will y'all be able to get out of there?" He flipped his wrist and glanced at his watch.

"We're on our way to the airport now. We got lucky. Our flight is the last one out of Miami. All the later flights had been canceled due to high winds.

"Not lucky. Blessed," Jami affirmed with a sigh of relief.

"Yes, daddy," Danica agreed, "I called mom, but her phone is going straight to voicemail."

Jami frowned, leaning against the banister. It was one thing not to answer his calls, but now, she was ignoring their daughters. The Harper he knew would never do that, but the Harper he *thought* he knew, no longer existed.

"I'll let her know."

"Hi, daddy," Kylie shouted in the background.

"Hey, baby girl. How are you holding up?"

"I'm fine. I'm worried about the locals and the tourists that won't be able to evacuate. The roads are already starting to backup. It's a good thing we left the hotel when we did or else we'd probably miss our flight," Kylie reflected, her voice filled with relief. "What are you and mom doing today?"

"I——*we*, are going hiking in the Great Smoky Mountains National Park." Jami glanced heavenward, then closed his eyes for a second.

The sound of steps in close proximity, crunching and scraping shifted Jami's focus to his surroundings. Aurora walked down the middle of the dirt and graveled road in his direction, pulling a four-wheeled trailer filled with janitorial supplies. She waved, giving him an award-winning smile, looking every bit of the country girl in brown cowboy boots, cut-off denim shorts, a red camisole, and an open plaid shirt with the sleeves rolled to her elbows.

"Hey there, Jamison," Aurora said, passing by.

He waved, feeling the corners of his lips lift upward.

"Who's that?" Kylie asked.

"The lady I rented the cabin from."

"No wonder she called you Jamison," Danica snickered, "it sounds weird. No one calls you by your government name unless it's business or a telemarketer."

"This is true," he replied, watching Aurora until she disappeared in the woods, more than likely on her way to clean a cabin for incoming guests.

"She has a friendly southern drawl," Kylie commented. "I hope mom doesn't get jealous."

If only...

"Your mom knows she's the only woman for me."

He believed that deep in his soul. Jami had loved Harper all of his life, and that reflex response rolled off just as natural as it had over the thirty years they've been together. Jami slid a hand in the pocket of his jeans, then glanced down at the backpack, his heart aching with the reminder of the sacrifice he made for Harper.

Jami purchased the non-refundable tickets in advance. He planned a full day in the mountains, and a romantic evening in the cabin. Although, Jami wasn't thrilled about the hike, he wasn't going to throw all of his money away.

"How close are y'all to the airport?" he asked, sitting on the steps.

"The GPS says we're ten minutes away," Danica replied.

"Call me when you board, and as soon as you land in Chicago, you here?"

"We will," Kylie said, "and don't worry dad, we're going to be okay."

"That's like telling a fireman not to run into a burning building——it's my job to worry," Jami countered, rubbing a hand up and down his thigh. "Be safe and get out of there. Love you both."

Ending the call, Jami sat on the steps, dropping his head between his knees. He closed his eyes and said a prayer for the girl's safe return home, and for all of those who didn't have the same opportunity to evacuate.

Jami kept up with storm data because he drove all over the southern states, and he needed to be prepared for the unknown as much as possible. Florida had tropical storms all the time, but Miami hadn't been hit with one since September 1926, during peak hurricane activity month. Aside for putting his daughters through school, the vehicle-mounted weather radar system attached to his rig was one of the best investments he made.

Sliding the tip of his middle finger across the phone screen, he stopped at Harper's contact, took a deep breath, then tapped on her name.

You have reached the voicemail box of Harper Wilcox.

Jami ended the call. Harper never turned her phone off. Never. She'd put it on silent, vibrate, or both when she didn't want to be disturbed, even when she was at work.

He called right back, and the voicemail greeted him again.

The phone never rang. Nothing. He winced. The bill was current, Jami was sure of that because he's the one that paid it.

Calling a third and a fourth time, rendering the same result, Jami placed the phone on the porch beside him. He stared off into the woods, dumbfounded. He didn't want to leave a voicemail. Disturbing news was better handled in person, but a phone call would have to do in this case.

"I'll be damned," he whispered as his chest burned with disbelief, causing his posture to stiffen. "She blocked me."

Getting to his feet, Jami called again, this time looking forward to the voicemail answering.

"You know, it's one thing to block me, but this——" He paused, checking his emotions. It didn't make sense for him to be irate. Harper made her intentions clear when it came to him. Jami took several deep breaths, then continued. "I know you're doing your own thing, but call me back. It's important. Call. Me. Back."

He waited a few minutes, willing the phone to ring. Jami was in such a state that he didn't see Aurora standing before him at the bottom of the steps.

"Jamison," she called out, waving her hands and tapping the step with her foot.

"Hey." He lifted his eyes from the phone.

"Are you all right? I'd called your name three times before I got for your attention." Aurora reached forward and slapped his brown and gray hiking boot. "Us southerners are friendly folks, but you can't zone out like that where I was able to walk up on you without you noticing," she warned.

Jami nodded, glancing at the phone again.

"What's wrong?" Aurora climbed the stairs and sat beside him.

"My daughters are in a precarious situation," Jami spewed, fighting the urge to dial Harper's number again. "They're okay, now, but the circumstances aren't good. I'm trying to reach their mother, and she's not answering," "It's not like her not to answer my calls or the girl's. I know things between us have changed, but——"

"Slow down." Aurora placed a hand on his knee. "Maybe there's a reason why she isn't picking up, especially if she's not answering your daughter's calls either."

Jami already knew Harper blocked his number, but didn't want to sound petty mentioning his theory to Aurora.

"Do you have any of her friend's numbers that are on the trip?"

"I do." Jami covered Aurora's hand and squeezed, then scrolled his contacts until he landed on Bianca Tremaine's number.

Jami and Bianca always had a cool friendship, mainly because she was married to his best friend.

"Hey, Bianca. It's Jami. Is Harper around?"

"Uhhh, hey——yeah."

"I wouldn't bother you if it wasn't important. I tried her phone, but I couldn't reach her."

"No problem. Hold on a minute."

Jami glanced over at Aurora and mouthed, "Thank you."

"Glad I could help," she replied, standing. "I'll give you

some privacy."

As Aurora trekked across the gravel roadway, he listened to the exchange between Bianca and Harper. He was appalled. Harper had the nerve to sound agitated as if he crossed the line calling Bianca.

Jami had the mind to hang up, and let Harper find out everything later. He didn't owe her the courtesy; their children were grown, but his innate reaction was to inform Harper. Jami had never been a half-assed parent and he wasn't going to start being one now, even though he didn't approve of Harper's actions.

Chapter 10

Heat rose from Harper's inner core, despite wearing only a bra, panties, and a white terry cloth robe. She crossed her legs like a toddler sitting in a circle for story time. DaJuan filled every waking thought; the same way he consumed her dreams. Why was her appetite for him so ravenous?

She reached for the emery board on the nightstand and filed her already perfectly manicured fingernails. She'd do just about anything to shift her adulterous thoughts from him. The massage and mimosas the women had scheduled in the next thirty minutes should do the trick.

"Jami's on the phone," Bianca said, bursting into Harper's room without knocking, wearing a matching robe.

Harper glanced over at her phone that laid on the nightstand. "Why would he be calling you?" She stopped mid swipe, dropping the emery board on the bed.

"He said he couldn't reach you. It sounds important." Bianca shoved the phone in Harper's face, then left the room, pulling the door closed behind her.

Harper waited a few seconds, then brought the phone to her ear. "What's going on?"

"Well, hello to you, too," Jami replied in a snarky tone. "I can't believe you blocked my number."

"What are you talking about?"

"I don't understand you. I've never blown your phone up when you were out, so why would I start now? If I'm calling repeatedly, you should know something's wrong, but I guess you wouldn't know anything since my calls are going straight to voicemail."

"Again, I don't know what you're talking about," Harper snapped, snatching her device from the nightstand with the charger still attached. "I didn't block your number. Why would I do that?"

"You tell me. It's not like you ever turn your phone off," Jami countered, sighing so hard that she could feel his exasperation. "What other reason would my calls go directly to voicemail without the phone ringing?"

Harper didn't give it much thought that her phone hadn't rang all morning. The people in her immediate circle knew she was on vacation. They were there with her. However, Harper did find it odd that she didn't hear any notification alerts from text messages, emails, or social media.

She turned the phone upright, pressing the home screen button several times. Nothing happened. "My phone's dead, but I don't know why. I plugged it in last night," Harper mumbled, leaning over the bed, peering behind the nightstand. The cord laid on the floor. "The plug wasn't pushed all the way in, or I pulled it out, either way, it's dead."

Harper made sure the cord was inserted in the base of the phone, then secured the opposite end into the outlet. A singular chirp sounded, then a red battery with a lightning bolt appeared on the black screen.

"I know I'm not your favorite person these days, but I would never block your number," Harper exclaimed, waiting for Jami to respond, but he didn't say anything. "I know you don't believe me."

After a slight pause, Jami replied, "I do."

Harper freed the breath she'd been holding, recognizing that she still sought Jami's approval——at least with some things. "What happened?"

"Let me start by saying, the girls are okay."

She sighed in relief, bracing herself for the rest of the conversation.

"A tropical storm will hit landfall in Miami tonight——"

"They don't leave until tomorrow." She hopped off the bed, falling to the floor with her foot twisted and trapped in the comforter. "How will they get home?"

"Harp——"

"What do they have in place for shelter?"

"Harp——"

"What category is it?"

Bianca and Michelle rushed into the room. "What happened?" Bianca asked, kneeling beside Harper, untangling the covers.

"How in the hell did you manage to fall out of the bed like that?" Michelle cracked, folding her arms across her full breasts that were spilling out of her robe.

"The girls are stuck in Miami and a hurricane is coming," Harper shrieked, getting to her feet, still holding the phone to her ear.

Michelle's grin fell flat.

"Oh my gosh." Bianca's hand flew to her mouth.

"Harper," Jami shouted, "listen to me. Harper."

"Yes," she pushed out, panting and clutching her chest.

"Danica and Kylie are okay. They should be at the airport by now and arriving home in a few hours."

"Huh?"

Bianca removed the phone from Harper's hands. "Hey, Jami. What's going on?"

Jami explained everything to Bianca. "Please make sure she's all right. I'll call if I hear anything else," he said right before ending the call.

Bianca slid the phone in the pocket of her robe as she turned to look at Harper. "The girls are fine."

"I know," Harper panted, sitting on the bed, flinching

from the insistent alerts that chimed on her phone, causing it to vibrate loudly across the nightstand.

Fumbling to grab it, Harper pressed the button. She had five missed calls from Jami, three from Danica, and two from Kylie. "No wonder he was pissed."

"Focus on the big picture, Harp," Bianca urged, sitting beside her.

Harper placed her head on Bianca's shoulder while going through the voicemails and texts. "At least he knew how to get ahold of me."

"I'm glad my goddaughter's are okay," Michelle said, tapping her wrist. "We have to get going or else we're going to miss our appointment."

Harper had lost track of the time. Her head was in mommy-mode, even though she knew the girls were fine. Guilt ate at her for missing their calls, especially after listening to the anxiety in their voices from the voicemails.

"Are you still up to going to our appointment?" Bianca asked.

"Yeah." Harper stood, slid the phone in her pocket, slipped on a pair of blingy flip-flops, and said, "Let's go."

The three of them moved at a fast pace toward the door, when three knocks greeted them. The ladies exchanged glances and expressions of bewilderment.

"Did one of y'all order room service?" Harper asked, moving closer to the door.

"Nah. I thought we were gonna have breakfast after our massages," Michelle replied.

"Who is it?" Harper asked, leaning in, looking through the peephole not able to see anyone's face.

"Mi ave a package fi Ms. Harpa," a masculine voice with an island accent responded.

"Damn." Michelle fanned herself. "Do all Jamaican men sound like they'll sweep you off your feet and make love to you with their voices alone? Wooo."

All Harper could do was stifle a laugh. She was thinking the same thing.

Bianca joined Harper, crossing her arms while arching an eyebrow. "Who's sending you gifts? Hmmmm."

"Probably from that fine young thang you had dinner with last night," Michelle added, standing on the opposite side of Harper, creating a devil on one shoulder and an angel on the other effect.

"Both of y'all hush." Harper smirked, opening the door.

"Gud day, ladies," the man said, entering their room, resembling a Jamaican Morris Chestnut, which meant he was a spitting image of Jami. "Weh yuh wudda like fi mi tuh sit it?"

"The counter is fine," Harper instructed as he placed the huge basket wrapped in cellophane down. She couldn't take her eyes off of him——his build, complexion, goatee——*Jamison Wilcox*.

Michelle walked around the man, scanning him from head to toe. "You wouldn't happen to have a brother you know nothing about living in Chicago?"

"Excuse mi?"

"Pardon my friend," Bianca grabbed Michelle by the hand,

yanking, and stepping in front of her. Then she angled a steely gaze at Harper.

"Oh. Yeah." Harper patted her pockets, then asked the man to wait a minute while she ran to the room to get his tip.

"That's nuh necessary."

"No. No. I insist," Harper countered, moving in the opposite direction.

"Ms. Harpa. No need Mr. DaJuan tell mi nuh fi tek yuh funds."

"What?" her head snapped, and her eyes shifted from Bianca to Michelle, then to the delivery man.

"Mr. DaJuan leave strict instructions," he said, moving toward the exit, and grabbing the doorknob. "Ave a gud day ladies."

"Well… someone is feeling you," Michelle commented, as they approached the basket.

Harper lifted the card, and read it aloud. *Thank you for a wonderful evening. Let me show you my island tonight. Wear a swimsuit. Meet me at our gazebo at five. DaJuan.*

"Our gazebo," Bianca teased.

"Girl hush." Heat traveled up the neck of the robe to her ears.

The cellophane crackled as Harper unwrapped the red ribbon. Blue Mountain Coffee, coffee liqueur, and gourmet sauces and spices filled the brown wicker basket. Harper inhaled as the rich aromas of the island flavors filled the room.

"This is nice and unexpected." Harper smiled, taking in DaJuan's thoughtfulness.

"Where do you suppose he wants to take you?" Bianca asked, as they left the room, and headed to the private beach area where they were scheduled to receive full-body massages.

"Probably to Negril. He told me how beautiful the beaches are there."

"He seems to be really into you," Bianca said, gazing at Harper.

"Wait a minute," Michelle interjected as they walked through the sand to a gazebo surrounded by palm trees on the opposite side of the resort. Three attendants dressed in white met them at the entrance. "Isn't Negril almost two hours away?"

"I think so, but I'm not going."

"Why not?" Michelle smirked, throwing her arm across Harper's shoulder. "You know you like him."

"Maybe——but that's not the point," Harper shot back. "For one, I'm not even sure that's where he's taking me. Secondly, every time I'm around him, my damn panties end up wet."

"What you say?" Bianca queried with an incredulous gasp.

"You've only seen him once," Michelle remarked, climbing the stairs onto the gazebo.

"He's been occupying my dreams. They're so damn real that I wake up horny."

"Well damn," Bianca and Michelle both exclaimed in unison.

"I'll go in your place if orgasms are on the menu, and all I have to do is look pretty," Michelle blurted out.

The three masseuses snickered, unable to hide their amusement.

Harper lowered her gaze to the wooden planks and shook her head.

Chapter 11

Jami nursed the steps for over an hour. His mind raced between thinking the worse about Harper, to giving her the benefit of the doubt, thanks to Aurora, to waiting to hear from his daughters.

"American made," Jami whispered, angling his head in the direction of the growling engine roaring nearby. He had an affinity for big trucks, which was one of the reasons he was drawn to his profession.

Seconds later, a metallic blue Chevy Tahoe pickup truck with oversized wheels pulled onto the parking pad next to

Jami's vehicle, and much to his surprise, Aurora was behind the wheel.

"Wow," Jami mumbled under his breath. There was something sexy about a woman driving a manly truck.

"What are you still doing here?" Aurora asked, sticking her head out of the window. "I thought you'd be in the Great Smokey's by now."

Jami missed the guided tour, but if he still wanted to go, he could venture off on his own.

"I'm going to hang around here until I hear from Danica and Kylie."

Aurora opened the door, jumping down from the high cabin, kicking up dust. "I can wait with you."

"That's not necessary. I'm sure you have plenty of things to do."

"That's not how we operate in these parts," she countered, coming toward him. "We see someone in need, we help them out. No questions asked."

"There's nothing you can do to fix this."

"Maybe not, but I can take your mind off of things for a little while," Aurora suggested, offering Jami a friendly smile, adjusting the rolled sleeves on the plaid shirt that slid below her elbows. "Let's go inside."

Jami glanced at her, cocking his head to the left. "For what?"

Aurora laughed, climbing the stairs, and hitting his arm. "I'm not propositioning you." She grabbed his heavy backpack and slung it over her shoulder like a feather. "You're just gonna have to trust me."

He followed Aurora inside, and stood in the living room as she moved around the cabin without any effort. Within minutes, she had half dozen board games, and two decks of cards in her arms. "What's your pleasure? Whichever you choose, I'm gonna come out victorious."

"Really now," Jami marched forward, taking the red deck of cards from the top of the pile. "Can you play spades?"

"Can you?" she questioned with a quirk of a well-trimmed eyebrow and a foxy grin.

Aurora placed the games on the cocktail table, then sauntered over to the kitchen island. She shoved a stool out with her foot toward Jami.

"Awe. Okay. It's on." He claimed the seat, taking the cards from the box, and tapping them on the counter so loud that the sound reverberated off the walls.

"Give me those." Aurora held out her hand, curling her fingers toward her chest. "First deal."

"I'm the guest, so I should be the one to choose." Jami angled his gaze and his eyebrows as if to ante up on Aurora's demand.

"House rules." Aurora winked, extending her arm across the counter.

"Mmmm hmmm." Jami placed the cards in her hand, admiring how she shuffled the deck, creating a bridge like a seasoned player. "Best three out of five."

"I usually play best two out of three, but if you need more chances to win, I'm cool with it," Aurora shot back, sitting the cards in the center of the counter. "Cut."

Jami nodded, feeling the corners of his lips curve to his jawline. He loved a woman who talked smack, and knew how to hold her own at the card table. The latter still remained to be seen.

Two hours, a bowl of popcorn, and a couple of glasses of wine later, they were deep into their tiebreaking game. Aurora had proven to be a worthy opponent, and could replace Trevor as his partner any day.

"I told you, I'm victorious." Aurora stood, flicking the nine of spades on the table, cutting Jami's ace of hearts. "You held onto that heart for dear life." She chuckled, doing a dance. "You thought I didn't have any more spades. I was trump tight."

"Yeah. Yeah." Jami rocked back on the stool, forgetting that there was no backrest, and losing his balance.

Aurora quickly grabbed a fistful of fabric in his chest, and yanked Jami forward. The force of the pull caused him to wrap both arms around the small of her back for support. Aurora's bountiful breast laid on his chest, and he inhaled her woodsy, but feminine fragrance.

Jami didn't move, and neither did she. Aurora glanced up at him, and whispers of her breath swept across his Adam's apple, releasing the sweet smell of sangria they'd been drinking. Ever so lightly, she kneaded his chest with the base of her hand, still clenching his shirt.

The slow gravitation of their lips meeting was painstakingly sensual, and worthy of being studied by actors as pointers for filming a love scene packed with anticipation.

Jami drew Aurora into him, and her hand traveled up, cupping the back of his head as their lips parted.

Just as their lips touched, Jami's phone rang, cutting the lustful tension between them.

"I'm sorry." He released Aurora for the first time, taking in the current situation, and retrieving the phone from the counter. "I have to get that."

"Of course," she relented, moving to the other side of the island, busying herself with the cards and used glasses.

"Danica."

"Hey, daddy. It's Kylie. We just landed."

"I can breathe now." Jami lowered onto the stool, careful not to lean back, glancing at the name displayed on the phone screen. It definitely said Danica. "When no one called to let me know if y'all made your flight, my thoughts were all over the place."

"Sorry about that. The security checkpoint was ridiculous, and we almost missed our plane. We literally had to run to the gate," Kylie explained, huffing. "I even lost my phone in the process, but I didn't have time to look for it."

"Don't worry about that. I'll buy you a new phone. Your life is more important."

"Thank you, daddy."

Jami could hear the happiness in her voice. Kylie was his baby girl——she was spoiled and she knew it. He didn't mind though, because Kylie worked hard at every task she took on, and always excelled.

"I have to go. Danica has a call coming in," Kylie said.

"You and mom have fun and I'll see you when you get home."

The joyful feeling in Jami's heart faded at the mention of Harper. The reality that the girls didn't know that she asked for a divorce weighed on him. No child, regardless of age, wants to hear that their parents are separating.

"Good news?" Aurora asked, claiming the stool next to Jami.

"Yes." He placed the phone on the counter, then wrung his hands. "I'm sorry about earlier. My behavior was out of line."

"Mine too," Aurora replied, sweeping strands of hair over her shoulder. "I got caught up in the moment, which is unacceptable and violates the morality clause that I put in place for my staff." Aurora slid off the stool, and made her way to the door. "I know better than to get involved with a guest. It won't happen again," she promised, twisting the knob and opening the door. "If you need something during the remainder of your stay, I'll send one of the workers over. Goodbye, Jamison."

He missed Aurora already, and she hadn't even crossed the threshold.

Chapter 12

Harper arrived at the gazebo an hour earlier than expected with Bianca and Michelle. She wore a string bikini with a sheer cover up that fell to her ankles with a long tantalizing split on the left side, showcasing one toned-brown leg up to her thigh.

"Funny how twenty-four hours can bring on a change," Harper remarked, taking in the scenery that had no resemblance of the previous night.

"What do you mean?" Bianca asked, leaning on the railing as the wind blew her flowing coral skirt like a flag.

"The area was set for a romantic dinner for two with all

the décor of a ballroom. The evening was quiet. The water was calm. DaJuan even planned our dinner so we could watch the sunset——it was breathtaking." Harper paused, remembering the beautiful earthy hues of last night's sky. "Now, there's nothing more here than the sea, which is a beautiful sight all its own, filled with swimmers, boaters, and thrill seekers on jet skis." She gazed out at the rippling waves. "I wonder what he has in mind."

"Sounds like Mr. DaJuan is full of surprises," Michelle commented, sliding a hand across the African waist beads that accentuated her pop-bottle frame. "Like, how did he know our room number?"

"I was wondering the same thing," Bianca said, facing them.

"I'm definitely going to ask, after I thank him of course, because I didn't give it to him," Harper responded, replaying the myriad of things they talked about last night. "Maybe the bellhop or the front desk clerk told him, either way, that's unacceptable."

The women ordered drinks, danced, and mingled with other tourists and natives that found their way to the gazebo while they waited. Harper grinned, eyeing Michelle having a private conversation in the corner with a guy named, Eldon, that they met earlier.

"Nice yacht," Harper commented to no one in particular as she gazed out into the sparkling water while polishing off the last of her piña colada.

"That's Mista Campbell," a beautiful brown-skin native

woman with thick wavy hair said, claiming the space next to Harper. "That's just one of fi him boats. Him ave tree."

"He must be pretty wealthy."

"Yea, him owns dis resort."

"When I grow up, I want to be just like Mr. Campbell," Bianca teased, bringing Harper another drink. "Working sixty hours a week as a criminal defense lawyer isn't where it's at. Or maybe, I should move my practice to Jamaica, defend criminals here, and soak up the sun and culture. My dollar will go further," Bianca said, smiling at Harper. "Then maybe——just maybe, I can buy myself a yacht, and we can have continuous vacations."

"I like the way you think." Harper nodded, holding up her drink, clinking glasses, then sipping their fruity cocktails.

"Hold on though." Bianca gazed out at the yacht. "Why does it look like he's moving in closer?"

Harper's attention drew to the yacht's bow that was only a few feet away from the gazebo. "None of the other boaters came over here."

"That's cuz dem nu have permission tuh dock here," the woman informed them, sauntering over, unlatching a lock in the gazebo, opening the fence, and tying the rope the crew tossed over to the dock.

"Gud afternoon, Mista Campbell," the woman greeted as he debarked the yacht.

"Holy shit," Harper mumbled under her breath, turning toward Bianca. "DaJuan is *Mr. Campbell?*"

"Gud afternoon, Kady." DaJuan smiled, and Harper insides

did that funny thing it does whenever she was around him.

"Damn Harp." Michelle rushed over. "Is that your young thang?"

"Yep."

"Don't look now, but he's coming over," Bianca warned in a low tone.

"Gud day ladies."

Bianca and Michelle returned the friendly greeting.

"Harper, it's so nice to see you again," DaJuan's said in a more sensual voice. One would have to be deaf not to notice the difference.

"Hey, DaJuan." She turned around slow and deliberate. "Nice to be seen."

"I'm a little early, but we can head out if that's okay with you?"

"Where are we going?" Harper asked, inhaling his wonderful scent that she'd grown to love.

"Beaches Negril on my yacht." He gestured toward the vessel.

"Is there enough room for two more?"

"Your friends are more than welcome, and Eldon too," DaJuan said, pointing at Eldon who was following up behind Michelle like a love struck puppy. "Eldon is a good friend of the family."

Everyone loaded the yacht, and off they went for a one and a half hour cruise, enjoying a smooth and stable ride along the Caribbean Sea. Kady was even on board, but Harper wasn't surprised. Kady probably knew who she was, all along. DaJuan played reggae music, and the staff served food and drinks on the main deck that housed a patio dining table set for six, and leather cushioned couches that lined the perimeter.

DaJuan took Harper's hand and lead her upstairs to the flybridge where Captain Williams steered the yacht.

"I will take it from here," DaJuan said to Captain Williams. "Go have some lunch and relax. I'll call if I need you."

"Thank you, Mr. Campbell," the Captain replied, removing his hat, and going downstairs.

"So, you know how to drive this thing?" Harper asked, gazing at DaJuan.

"I do, but you're going to be the one at the helm."

"Are you kidding me? I can't steer this ship."

"I will show you," DaJuan said, guiding Harper until she stood at the helm of the yacht, then situated himself behind her, leaving no room between them.

Harper's breath quickened at the feel of his mid-section touching her rear.

"Why is the steering wheel so big?" *That wasn't the only thing she wanted to question the large size of.*

"For better control. You can steer from either side of the yacht," DaJuan explained, reaching around Harper to the control panel. "I'm going to drop the speed to eight knots, and you will do the rest."

"Okay."

DaJuan leaned in, resting the side of his face close to her ear, then whispered, "You look extra pretty today."

Harper's entire body trembled and there was no faking the

movement. She hoped he didn't address it. "Thanks."

She held onto the wheel, and DaJuan stayed behind her while she steered the yacht. Harper felt powerful and in control … of the vessel. Her hormones were a different story.

The whitest sand and the clearest water she'd ever seen appeared before them. "This is beautiful."

"Seven Mile Beach is like no other beach in Jamaica."

Harper laid her head back on DaJuan's broad chest, continued to get drunk on his scent, steered the yacht, and relished the view.

Uptown Funk by Bruno Mars, played muffled in the background.

"This is my jam. It's one of those songs that makes you want to dance whenever you hear it." Harper bounced to the beat. "I didn't know you liked Bruno Mars."

"I do, but I'm not playing it," DaJuan replied, bouncing in sync with Harper. "Sounds like it's coming from your bag."

The song ended, then started again.

"That's my phone." Harper reached into her bag with the long cross-body strap. "Give me a sec, that's my daughter," she said, anxious to speak with her girls. "Hey, Danica. Have you and Kylie made it home yet?"

"Why is Uncle Eric and EJ moving your things?"

Harper bit her bottom lip and covered her face.

"Everything all right?" DaJuan inquired, grabbing the wheel.

"Who's that?" Danica asked in a tone that she shouldn't be using with her mother. "Is he the reason you're moving out?

Where's dad?"

Harper waved DaJuan off, shoving him to the side, nearly knocking him on his rear. She marched at a fast-pace down the steps, passing by her friends, Captain Williams, and the rest of the staff, to the front of the ship where she could speak in private.

All of Harper's belongings were supposed to be moved into her new apartment before the girls returned from Miami. She kicked herself for not following her first mind to leave Jami back in January. The girls had just returned to campus after Christmas break, and Harper would have had the time to get settled in her new place. She planned to tell them when they came home for spring break in March, but the attorney advised Harper not to make any sudden moves until the paperwork was finalized. Why did she listen to her?

"Ma. Are you and daddy getting a divorce?"

"What did your uncle tell you?"

"Nothing. He told me to talk to you. Why are you moving out?"

"That's between me and your father."

"This affects me and Kylie too. I can't believe you just said that to me.

"Harper, I'm worried about you," DaJuan expressed, sneaking up from behind, causing Harper to flinch, dropping her phone into the Caribbean Sea.

"Look what you made me do," she shouted, grabbing hold of the railing.

"I didn't mean any harm."

"Whatever." Harper stormed to the rear of the boat where everyone was gathered, then made a sharp turn, going into the guest cabin below deck. She plopped on the king-size bed wrapped in brown marble casing and cream accents that sat in the center of the room.

"What the hell did you do to her?" Michelle yelled.

"Nothing."

"She wasn't like that a few minutes ago. What the hell did you do?"

"Nothing, I swear."

"You stay right there," Michelle ordered, then Harper heard several pairs of feet moving quicker than a marching band, stomp down the stairs.

Michelle and Bianca entered the cabin, closing the door behind them.

Harper glanced in their direction as the dam broke, soaking her thighs with tears. Bianca snatched facial tissues from the built-in vanity, then rushed to her side, moving the braids from Harper's face.

She didn't feel regret for her decision to leave. The tears might have indicated sadness to those around Harper, but they were from embarrassment and humiliation.

"I'm going to——" Michelle spun around, grabbing the doorknob.

"DaJuan didn't do anything," Harper whispered, wiping her face.

"Then, why are you crying?" Michelle asked, occupying the seat beside Harper.

Bianca rubbed her back, easing some of the tension that took over Harper's body and emotions.

After a few quiet moments, Harper said, "The girls know about me and Jami. Well, they know I've moved out. I don't think they've talked to their dad yet——matter of fact, I know Danica hasn't because of the questions she was asking me."

"Oh, honey," Bianca whispered in a soothing tone. "You need to call Jami and give him a heads up."

"I can't." Harper stood, walking to the other side of the room. "My phone is at the bottom of the sea."

Michelle squinted, tilting her head.

"DaJuan startled me and I dropped it overboard."

"Here." Bianca handed Harper her phone, then she and Michelle left the room.

Harper scratched her head, and blew out a breath between pursed lips. Miscommunication, assumptions, and turmoil had taken over her vacation, and she had no one to blame but herself.

She released an exaggerated breath, dialing Jami's number. Harper wasn't looking forward to speaking with him, particularly not about this.

"Hey, Jami. Danica knows I moved out."

"I'm aware," he replied, sighing into the receiver. "I'm getting an earful on the other line."

Harper plopped down on the bed. "I'm sorry things are transpiring like this. I never meant to hurt you or them."

"Yet, here we are," Jami mumbled in that tone Harper had gotten accustomed to over the years, where whatever Jami was thinking slipped out unintentionally.

"If you need to reach me, call Bianca's phone. I lost mine," she said, clearing her throat. "I'll call Danica and explain. You shouldn't have to clean up my mess."

"True, but not necessary. I told Danica we would discuss things as a family when we returned home," he countered with a chuckle that was off-putting. "By the way, who's this man that Danica thinks you're cheating on me with?"

Chapter 13

"Harp, we're headed to the Freemont Shopping Centre. Do you want to come? Bianca asked, standing in the doorway of Harper's room.

"I'm good here," she replied, sadness coloring her voice as she flipped through the channels on the remote.

"It's been two days." Bianca closed the door, claimed the spot next to Harper on the bed, and took the remote out of her hands. "How much longer are you going to stay held up in this room, punishing yourself?"

Harper rolled over, facing Bianca. "I don't feel like

being around people right now. My whole life is a mess." She sighed, digging her head further into the down pillow. "I don't know which is worse——Danica's continuous calls to Jami, demanding answers or Kylie, who refuses to speak to me at all. Danica thinks I'm avoiding her, even though her dad told her that I lost my phone. Every time Jami texts to let me know, I can hear the disappointment in the tone of his message."

"I know things aren't the best, but you can't stay in this unhealthy headspace. Come out, get some fresh air, and enjoy the last three days of our trip. Your problems may not seem so overwhelming if you free your mind for a bit."

Harper knew Bianca was right, but she remained quiet.

"You made a decision that was best for you, and although the girls don't approve, this is between you and Jami. Your relationship is y'all's business," Bianca reminded her, pulling the covers back. "You're coming with us and I'm not taking no for an answer."

Thirty minutes later, Harper and Bianca met Michelle in the lobby. She was having a drink with Eldon, wearing the most telling grin.

Michelle had spent the past couple of nights in Eldon's suite. However, she still managed to keep the daily scheduled plans with Bianca and Harper——well with Bianca since Harper had checked out on them. Nevertheless, Harper was happy for her friend.

"I wasn't sure if you would join us," Michelle said, sliding off the stool and hugging Harper. "I'm glad you did. Nothing like retail therapy——Jamaican style to lift your spirits."

Michelle dipped, rotating her hips like a belly dancer.

"Will I see you later?" Eldon asked, mimicking Michelle's sultry movements.

Harper and Bianca shared a glance.

"You'll just have to wait and see," Michelle teased, batting her eyelashes.

"Who does Michelle think she's fooling?" Harper whispered, leaning in close to Bianca. "She's dissing us at night for the remainder of this trip."

"I know right." Bianca giggled, unable to contain her laughter.

***

"Thanks for dragging me out," Harper expressed to Bianca and Michelle as they sauntered through the hotel lobby with numerous shopping bags. "This is just what I needed."

"To max out your Visa," Michelle shot back, jokingly. "You're going to need another suitcase to bring all of that stuff back home."

"I always come prepared," Harper countered, swinging the bags, hitting Michelle on the backside. "I packed an extra duffel for this reason."

They were a few steps shy of the elevator when Harper stopped unexpectantly, and inhaled. The intoxicating masculine scent she'd grown to love infused her nostrils, causing every nerve ending in her body to tingle. Before she could react, he called out her name. Bianca's finger stopped mid-press of the elevator button, and Michelle turned around, noticing that Harper was no longer beside her.

Harper swallowed past the lump in her throat as she turned around. DaJuan stood an arm's length away, looking more handsome than she remembered in a suit and bowtie, carrying a small iridescent shopping bag.

"Hi, beautiful. I haven't seen you in a few days."

"You know what suite I'm in," Harper countered, fighting the urge to smile. "Seeing as though you own this resort and have had things messengered to me." She didn't want DaJuan to know how happy she was to see him too.

"I thought about coming to your suite," DaJuan replied under hooded eyes. "But I didn't think you would appreciate me showing up to your room uninvited."

"True."

"Besides, we didn't leave things on a positive note." He paused, stepping in a little closer. "I wasn't sure you wanted to see me."

"We're going up," Bianca announced, sticking her arm in the elevator door.

"Hold on," Harper said, then put her focus back on DaJuan. "Would you like to come up?"

"I'd love too." He relieved Harper of her bags, then followed her onto the elevator. "Good day, ladies," DaJuan spoke, his voice shaky.

"Don't worry. I'm not going to snap at you again," Michelle teased, making room. "Harper explained what happened."

"Good," he replied, releasing a deep sigh. "I felt like

Killmonger under attack by the Dora Milaje female warrior troupe in Black Panther."

Everyone chuckled.

"We always have each other's back," Harper said, and Bianca and Michelle nodded.

"Just know that you'll never have to watch your back with me. I'll keep you safe," DaJuan countered in a tone so smooth, leaving Harper with nothing intelligent to say. She kept her naughty thoughts to herself.

They entered the suite, and Bianca and Michelle ventured off to their rooms, closing the doors.

"Where would you like for me to sit these?"

"The counter is fine."

Harper dropped her purse on the sofa, then proceeded to the private balcony that overlooked the water. She sank into one of the wicker chairs with plush cushions, and kicked off her sandals.

"Nice view ... and I'm not talking about the scenery." DaJuan flirted, joining Harper and handing her the shopping bag.

Again, he left her speechless.

"I didn't know if you were team iPhone or android, so I purchased both."

Harper took the rectangular iPhone box out, and gave DaJuan back the bag. "Thank you."

"That's the least I could do. I didn't mean——"

"You don't have to say another word." Harper angled her body toward him. "I had a lot going on, and took my frustrations out on you. The phone falling overboard was the final straw that made me lose it. I'm sorry."

DaJuan bit the corner of his bottom lip, scooting the matching chair closer to Harper. He lowered onto the cushion, then lifted Harper's legs by the ankles, and placed them in his lap. She closed her eyes, and sunk further into the seat as he massaged and kneaded her feet.

"Let me take your worries away for the rest of your trip," he whispered, applying just the right amount of pressure to the middle of her foot with one hand, while rotating her toes with the other.

A moan escaped deep from the back of Harper's throat. DaJuan was hitting all of the pressure points, relaxing every muscle in her body. Harper didn't know if she was in a vulnerable state or if she just didn't care anymore, but she released her inhibitions and agreed.

***

For the next three days, DaJuan catered to Harper as if she were his woman, and she enjoyed every minute of the special attention. They spent time on Beach Negril, shopping, eating fine cuisine, and an afternoon at his family's home, which was livelier than any party she'd ever attended.

Dinner on DaJuan's yacht in the middle of the Caribbean at sunset was her absolute favorite, as well as waking up in his arms to watch the sunrise. She loved the intimacy they shared, without having to take their clothes off.

She even told him about Jami and why she left the marriage. He listened without judgement, giving her his full attention.

***

"I see you," Michelle teased, checking out Harper's outfit. "You're leaving nothing to the imagination for your last night with DaJuan."

Harper wore a sleeveless mermaid, open back, red sequin evening gown with a plunging neckline. The celebrities on the Hollywood red carpet had nothing on her.

"When did you pick up this sexy number?" Bianca asked.

"Yesterday, DaJuan took me to a designer dress boutique, handed me his Amex Black card, and told me to buy any evening gown and accessories I wanted."

"Nice," Bianca commented, straightening the floor-length train. "I'm thrilled to see you smiling and happy."

"It feels damn good to be desired," Harper replied, releasing a pleasing sigh. "This is what I've been missing the last several years in my marriage, and though it's temporary, I will cherish every moment."

A knock at the door, halted any further conversation.

Harper gave herself a quick once-over in the mirror, then proceeded to the entrance. The butterflies in the pit of her stomach fluttered as she drank in the handsome specimen who stood before her. She couldn't help but smile.

"You look absolutely breathtaking," DaJuan said, stepping inside. His eyes glistened with lust, taking Harper by the hand, circling her like a merry-go-round. "I can't believe this is our last night together."

"I can't believe I've wasted the time we could've had together, worrying if I should trust my instincts," Harper admitted, not caring that she put her feelings out in the open. "I'm going to miss you."

"Let's not worry about what we missed, and let's focus on the time we have right here. Right now." DaJuan moved in, sweeping her braids aside, and kissing the nape of Harper's neck. "I have a special evening planned for us."

"Where are we going?"

"It's a surprise," he whispered, nuzzling his nose along Harper's ear, making her insides perform a sensual rumba.

She touched his cheek, guiding his face in front of hers until their eyes connected. DaJuan placed his forehead against Harper's, pecking her lips, still holding that passionate gaze into her soul. DaJuan knew exactly what he was doing, and Harper was going to let him have his way with her tonight.

Chapter 14

Jami had five days left at the cabin, and he had no desire to stay there. The constant reminders of the ways he planned on pleasing Harper stared him in the face——the pool table, the private Jacuzzi outback, and the upslope stretch chaise lounge. However, those reminders bothered him a little less with each passing day.

However, what nagged him more than that, was not seeing Aurora. She made the first couple of days manageable, and to his surprise——enjoyable. He missed her lighthearted nature, the smell of her hair, her laugh, and the way she saw the good in the bleakest of situations.

He spent the next couple of days, sightseeing, and on the third day, he checked out of the cabin, booking his last three days at a five-star hotel.

While loading the last of his items in the trunk, he spotted Aurora across the way, pulling a couple of tin bear receptacles to the edge of the roadway. His heartbeat accelerated, making his feet move in Aurora's direction before his brain registered what he was doing.

"Let me help you with that."

"Hey," she said, giving a smile that didn't quite reach her eyes.

Jami didn't care. He knew it had more to do with the compromising predicament at the cabin a few nights ago, than her not being happy to see him. Aurora looked cute in an everyday girl next door kind of way, wearing baggy jean overalls, a checkered tube top, a gray vintage baseball cap with a long braid hanging down her back, and dusty black Timberlands.

"I received your email this morning," Aurora commented, gripping the straps on the overalls. "I hope our encounter had nothing to do with you checking out early."

"It played a role, but not in a bad way." He paused, registering the confusion on her face. "I'm not leaving Sevierville——just the cabin. I booked a room at a hotel about two miles away."

"That doesn't make any sense."

"I enjoy spending time with you, and I can't do that as

long as I'm a guest here."

"Jamison, I don't think that's a good idea," she countered, looking everywhere but his eyes. "Your situation——"

"Is not one of my making, and yes, I was a mess on that first night." He moved in a little closer. "But that doesn't change the fact that I miss your company. Your candor. Your vibe. I want a chance to get to know you better. Are you open to that?"

Aurora's shoulders heaved as she panted, removing the gray hat, and fanning herself. Two short chirps pierced the air, snatching both of their attention to the car passing by.

"That's the couple in cabin four." She smiled and waved, turning her back to Jami, watching the car drive away. "They're really nice people."

Jami waited a few seconds to see if she would acknowledge his question. The connection they shared was unexpected, and in his heart, he knew Aurora felt it too. *What other reason would she have to hesitate?*

"You don't have to give me an answer right now," Jami said which caused Aurora to face him. "I'm a patient man. But do know, I'm not leaving Tennessee until I have a chance to spend time with you." He took a step backward. "I'll be in touch."

Jami returned to the cabin, giving the space another sweep. He did a thorough check before loading the truck, but a second look never hurt. He stopped, glancing at the kitchen island where he and Aurora almost shared a kiss, then snickered. Jami wondered if he would've been able to control himself had their tongues united.

Satisfied with his search, he stepped onto the porch and was stunned to see Aurora standing at the bottom of the stairs.

"Hey."

"I thought about it," Aurora said, swaying side to side. "And——I'd love to hang out with you."

"Cool." He came forward. "Let me check in and get settled, and I'll pick you up at eight."

A smile split her face as wide as the Great Smoky Mountains, putting Jami's nerves at ease.

"What should I wear?"

"Casual attire——jeans, sneakers, sandals. Whatever you feel most comfortable in."

***

Jami pulled into Strike Out Lanes parking lot.

"I'm going to challenge your competitive spirit. Let's see how well you throw a ball."

Aurora beamed. "I love bowling. You should've told me ahead of time. I would've brought my gear, but don't worry. I'll beat you with a house ball and raggedy rental shoes."

"This is going to be a fun night." Jami grinned, rubbing his hands together, exiting the car, then coming around to open Aurora's door.

The crashing sound of bowling balls slamming into the pins, loud talking, boisterous laughter, and music greeted them upon entry.

"Hey, girl. What are you doing here on a Wednesday night?"

a tall woman with large hoop earrings behind the service desk inquired, glancing at Jami with an inquisitive smile.

"Hanging out with my friend, Jamison."

He waved.

"Are lanes one and two open?" Aurora asked, standing on her tiptoes, looking to her far right.

The woman turned her attention to the computer screen. "No one likes bowling on the wall other than you."

"You're a regular, huh?" Jami smirked, pulling a credit card from his wallet.

"Something like that," Aurora shot back, and the woman snickered, and shook her head.

Jami tried to give the woman his card, but she refused to take it. "Your money's no good here as long as you're with her."

"Oh. Well, excuse me." He held his hands in the air.

"Have a good night, LaRue." Aurora slipped a finger in the beltloop on Jami's jeans. "Come on."

"Thanks, boss lady," LaRue responded before taking care of the next customer.

"I learn more about you every second," he said as they walked to lanes one and two. "You own this establishment?"

"It's a family business. I'm the fifth generation, and when or if I have children, I'll pass it on to them. If not, it'll go to my baby brother's children."

"That's great. Keep the generational wealth and entrepreneurship going."

Sooner than Jami realized, they had bowled four games,

devoured a party tray of hot wings, and drank a couple of beers. Endless laughter and conversation consumed them, making Jami feel like they were the only people in the house.

"I don't appreciate you beating up on me." He frowned, looking at the final score. "How do you bury the ball in the pocket and end up with a seven-ten split? I'm convinced. You got it rigged. I was coming for you, and you put a jinx on the pins."

"Don't be a sore loser." Aurora wiggled his knee, her touch awakening all the nerves in his body.

"Never that." Jami winked, eyeing the billiards area. "Are you up for a game of pool?"

"Sure, but just so you know, eight ball is my game."

"Bring it. I'm about to put an end to this madness." He cleaned their area, then changed his shoes, and grabbed hers. "I'll be back."

"Where're you going?"

"To turn these in, and pay for table time."

"You don't have to do that."

"I know, and that's why I'm going to do it. Put the money in your petty cash, the bar's tip jar, or whatever."

"Jamison——"

"I'm a man baby. Let me do what I do."

Aurora surrendered, gazing at him, then whispered, "You're nothing like my ex-husband. He was always looking for a handout."

"I'm not like most men," he declared, then held up an index finger. "Correction. I *am* like most *men*. Us good guys outweigh the bad, but they're the ones that you always hear about, skewing the perception."

"I'll be glad when I experience one on a deeper level. My husband was supposed to be my forever, you know?"

Jami claimed the seat next to her, placing the shoes on the floor.

"No one foresees their marriage not lasting," he said, reflecting on him and Harper. "Sometimes things happen and we may not know why at that moment, but I'm sure clarity will come … at least I'm praying it will."

"It will. You can't force someone to love you or stay where they no longer want to be for whatever reason. All you can do is accept that you did your best, and move on," Aurora advised, putting on a pair of low top canvas sneakers. "For me, divorce was the best outcome. My life is much better. I didn't envision things turning out this way, however, I'm glad they did."

Nodding, Jami absorbed her words of wisdom, then shook off the ill feelings that the thought of Harper carried.

"Let's get this butt whipping started." Jami grabbed their shoes to return them to the front desk. "I'll meet you in the billiards room."

"Loser racks the balls," Aurora blurted out.

"That's fair."

Another hour had passed, and Jami could finally claim victory. He'd beaten Aurora all three games. He tried not to boast, but his ego wouldn't let that happen.

"Victorious one, your winning streak is over." Jami spun, holding onto the wooden stick, then flipped on his tiptoes like

Michael Jackson. "You played a good game, but mine was better."

"It's about time," she teased, racking the balls, then reaching for Jami's cue stick.

He held it close to his chest. "Let me show you something," he said, moving beside Aurora, lifting the pool rack triangle, and placing the white cue ball behind the head string. "You have a superb game, but your form needs a little work. You correct that, and you'll be deadly." Jami glanced over at Aurora, and he could see the wheels churning. "Keep your eyes focused on my stance and the alignment of my chin with the cue ball."

Jami got low, then with powerful precision, he hit the cue ball, pocketing three solids and one stripe.

"Show me again."

Handing Aurora the cue stick, he moved directly behind her. "Line up your shot. Since you're righthanded, place your right foot underneath the back of your cue stick, Jami advised, touching Aurora's outer thigh. "Then set your left foot about forty-five degrees apart."

Aurora adjusted her stance. "Like this?"

"No." Jami splayed his fingers across Aurora's hips, placing his leg between hers, and pushing her left foot out a little further. Then, he shifted her hips until they were at the correct angle. "Like this," Jami said, his tone more husky than before.

Placing a hand on the small of her back, Jami gently pushed Aurora forward. He mirrored her position, but thrusted his hips back so they wouldn't touch. He'd have a hard time explaining why all of the blood had rushed down to his midsection, causing a bulge in his pants.

"Keep a steady balance, get low, and line your chin over the cue stick." Jami backed away, adjusting himself while he had a chance to do it discreetly. "When ready, shoot your shot."

***

The next day, Aurora sabotaged Jami's plans to go to Forbidden Caverns, and took him to Dollywood Theme Park in Pigeon Forge, Tennessee. They rode rollercoasters, played games, and got their faces painted like a couple of high school kids.

"I haven't had this much fun in a very long time," Jami admitted as they strolled through the amusement park, eating hot dogs and drinking sweet tea. "My life is so routine and it's hard to carve out moments where I can let loose and not feel drained, or feel guilty for being drained."

"I get it. Maintaining the cabins and running Strike Out Lanes consume much of my free time," Aurora added, chuckling. "My ma told me that I'll never find another husband if I don't stop working like a mad woman and put myself out there."

"She didn't mince any words." Jami tossed his trash in the can off to the side.

"Ma never does. I told her that work *is* my husband."

"That must be lonely." Jami hooked his pinky finger around Aurora's, and she curled her finger, securing the grip.

"You deserve to be loved."

Aurora released his pinky, and interlocked all of her fingers with Jami's. "And so do you."

Chapter 15

"What are you doing?" Harper asked, watching DaJuan insert a key into a maintenance control panel in the elevator.

He opened a small steel door, then pressed a code on the keypad. Immediately, her feet felt heavy as the elevator rose. Harper's breath quickened when DaJuan flashed his gorgeous smile, disarming her. He never uttered a word, and without warning, DaJuan slipped a scarf over her eyes and tied it behind her head.

"I've never been blindfolded before," Harper admitted, touching the lustrous silk fabric. "Can I trust you?"

"What does your gut say?" he asked, lifting Harper's hands from her face, interlocking their fingers.

Pushing out a slow breath, she responded, "Yes."

A soft chime pierced the air as the ride came to a halt. Still holding Harper's hand, DaJuan guided her off the elevator. Her heels echoed with every step she took, giving the impression of being in an empty room or hollow space.

"Watch your step," DaJuan cautioned, squeezing her hand. "There's three shallow stairs for you to climb."

"Is this your private penthouse suite? Is that why you needed to punch in a secret code?"

DaJuan laughed in a way that revealed he was up to something.

"Well, it *is* the top floor."

There he goes again being presumptuous ... but who was she fooling, Harper wanted him too.

She heard a door creak open and was immediately taken aback from a loud swooshing sound, and the sudden uptick of wind encircling her body. The warm air caressed Harper's skin, causing her nipples to harden. She hoped DaJuan didn't notice, or if he did, he'd be a gentleman and not say anything. She'd have to trust that he didn't since she couldn't see.

DaJuan kissed her cheek, freeing Harper from her thoughts. He brushed her arm and hip as she felt him move behind her. The closeness of his body made her even warmer. Six days ago, Harper fought those feelings, but now she welcomed them.

He unknotted the scarf, and Harper's insides beamed probably matching the expression she knew shown on her face. However, she did her best to play it cool.

A pearl white helicopter with sleek aerodynamic lines sat

on the helipad. The beautiful machine reminded Harper of going to the Chicago Auto Show back home. Tons of concept cars, domestic and imported passenger vehicles were on display. Although, the helicopter was an aircraft, its futuristic design was topnotch like the vehicles she admired at the coveted show.

"Wow," she said under her breath.

DaJuan wrapped his arms around her waist, resting his head on her shoulder, standing cheek to cheek. "Are you ready for our adventure?"

Harper nodded, unable to speak in the moment.

He lightly pressed his middle to her backside, nudging Harper forward. They ambled to the helicopter. Soon as they made it to the door, it slid open.

"Good evening Mr. DaJuan and Ms. Harper," a man greeted in all white attire, extending a hand to Harper.

"After you," DaJuan gestured as she placed a hand in the gentlemen's. DaJuan held the other hand until she got her footing, and then hopped in the helicopter.

Harper's senses detected the inimitable aroma of jerk chicken, piquing her interest as she took in the surroundings. The cabin was even more impressive than the exterior, decked out in white leather and caramel marble with matching plush carpet. Two oversized media room sofa seats sat opposite each other with a wraparound couch in the back, and something draped with a white tablecloth in the center. She guessed that was the cuisine that made her stomach growl in anticipation.

She claimed a seat, feeling like an a-list celebrity on her way to perform at the Grammy Awards making a special entrance. "This is nice."

"I told you we were on the top floor." He grinned, sitting across from her.

"Yeah … you did." Harper swiveled the seat until she was facing DaJuan. "So, what else do you have planned?"

"Netflix and chill," he teased.

Harper was shocked he was familiar with that millennial saying, thinking it was only an American thing.

"More like dinner and a movie," DaJuan caved, giving a crooked grin that dripped with sexiness.

"I'm looking forward to it." Harper leaned back, angling her legs, crossing them at the ankles. That's all the fitted mermaid dress would allow. "It smells delicious."

***

The next hour, the server catered to their needs, and when done, he activated the blackout and soundproof partition, and joined the pilot in the cockpit. They enjoyed the breathtaking aerial Jamaican views while cuddling on the couch as their hands explored each other's body through their clothing. Harper was so engulfed with simmering heat that she couldn't take much more of the teasing.

"Kiss me. Slow and passionate," Harper said, her voice throaty and filled with aching desire. "Kiss me like you'll never see me again." She panted, tracing his lips with her finger. "Kiss me like you're being shipped off to war, and you want me to remember what you taste like."

DaJuan gazed into her eyes so deep that Harper saw her reflection. He stroked her face with the gentleness of handling a newborn, then his fingers found their way to her braids. DaJuan grabbed a fistful, and tugged her hair, lifting her chin to meet his lips. He kissed her just as she instructed.

Harper's insides moistened and her heart thumped with a greedy hunger. The more she moaned, the further he went. DaJuan tasted and nipped the skin along Harper's neck and shoulder, sliding a hand behind her back, unzipping her gown, and peeling it down just below her bosom. She didn't stop him.

Leveling the playing field, Harper relieved DaJuan of his suit jacket and button-down shirt. His broad, firm, and smooth chest excited her, causing Harper to entangle her fingers in his locs until the updo style fell, sweeping the sides of his face, tickling her breasts.

DaJuan massaged her ample mounds and feasted on her nipples. Anxious to see what he was working with, Harper freed the bulge pressing against his zipper.

"One moment." DaJuan adjusted, pulling a wallet from his pocket, retrieving a condom.

She was grateful that he had the foresight to bring protection. Harper couldn't remember the last time she had to purchase any. She'd been with the same man her entire life.

DaJuan peeled Harper's dress off, gasping, touching her bare private areas that should've been covered with underclothing. Her evening attire left no room for them, not even a stringy thong.

"You're so beautiful," he mumbled, circling her navel

with his tongue, gripping the back of her thighs, then pulling Harper onto his lap.

She straddled him, and DaJuan entered Harper. Her muscles contracted, welcoming him as he filled Harper completely. She felt intense delight as they fed their feverish appetites that had built up over the weeks' time. Harper wasn't a quiet lover when in the throes of passion. Jami had told her that, especially trying to stay silent while having sneaky sex when their daughters were younger. Tonight's rendezvous with DaJuan was no exception.

"Mr. DaJuan, unless otherwise instructed, we will be landing in the next twenty minutes," the captain announced over the intercom. "Please fastened your seatbelts."

"Thank you," he replied, pressing a button on the wall.

Harper shot a glance at DaJuan, reaching for her dress. "I thought they couldn't hear us."

"Only if I leave this in the upright position," he explained, pointing to the switch above the button he pressed. "I promise, no one else heard your cries of pleasure, but me."

She gave him a flirty side-eye, taking his hand. DaJuan escorted Harper to the bathroom that was just as exquisite as the cabin, showing her where the towels were so she could freshen up.

"Oh my——the mountain tops are *blue*," Harper gasped, walking into the cabin, claiming her seat, and buckling in. "If I didn't see this with my own eyes, I'd swear this was an optical illusion. Where are we?"

"The Blue Mountains in Saint Thomas."

"I know I sound like I'm on repeat, but this is so beautiful."

"You expressed how much you loved nature in its natural state the first night we had dinner. Do you remember that?"

"Yes." She grinned, surprised that he remembered.

Harper heard her mother's voice, dropping gems. *Men have a way of zoning in on a woman's wants, needs, and desires when they are truly interested and value the woman. Don't settle on a man who misses the everyday little things that make up you.* Harper smiled at the memory, trying to block out the final statement. *Jami's a good man. I'm happy you have someone who loves you the way he does.*

"What's that huge white thing?" she asked as the helicopter descended. "It looks like a theater sized movie screen on steroids."

"I did say dinner *aaand a movie.*"

"On top of the mountain?" she gasped, taking in the scenery, eyeing a tent, picnic-style blanket, pillows, and basket.

"It's the best place to enjoy the view."

"I should've known you'd plan something like this," Harper commented, carefully stepping out of the helicopter. "Every place we've been, you've somehow incorporated spectacular scenic backdrops."

They ate fruit, drank wine, and made love in the tent while the movie, How Stella Got Her Groove Back, played in the background. The irony wasn't lost on Harper. By the time they finished ravishing each other, the credits were rolling.

"Great movie," Harper teased, dragging an index finger down the middle of his chest.

DaJuan chuckled, running a hand through Harper's braids.

She grabbed his wrist, halting his movement. "I hope you're not trying to tell me you're as young as Winston in the movie."

"If I was, it's too late to have any regrets." DaJuan laughed, pulling Harper to him. "You put it on this young man."

Harper couldn't imagine having relations with someone younger than her daughters. But she didn't regret a damn thing. DaJuan handled her body like an experienced lover, and Harper's insides continued to quiver, and she enjoyed every tingle and twinge.

"I'm thirty-six," DaJuan confessed.

"And I'm hungry for more," she replied, pulling him on top of her. On demand, DaJuan's manhood rose to the occasion.

Chapter 16

"No more surprises," Jami told Aurora, dropping her off at the cabin after they had breakfast at the diner. "I'm taking charge of our date tonight."

"Duly noted," Aurora replied as Jami got out of the truck, then came around to open her door. "Casual attire?"

"More like a night out on the town attire. Grown folks style." Jami paused, gazing at Aurora. "We're going dancing."

The corners of her lips lifted into a full smile. "I love it."

Four hours later, Jami pulled in front of Aurora's cabin, eager to spend the evening with her. He was astounded how a woman he'd just met, had brought him so much joy. Turning his head to spot the moment Aurora opened the door, Jami caught a glimpse of himself smiling in the rearview mirror. It had been a while since a woman made him giddy, and he welcomed the feeling.

Reflecting on the meaningful conversations and time they've spent together, Jami felt like he knew Aurora better than he'd known Harper. Jami's always been a believer that all things happened for a reason, but how could the failure of his marriage be a good thing?

Seconds later, Aurora stepped onto the porch. Jami gulped, clenching his teeth as he swirled his tongue around to produce moisture in his mouth. Aurora was a natural beauty. He noticed that the first day they met, but seeing her all dolled-up, evoked a different set of feelings that he couldn't put into words. Rushing out of the truck, he couldn't peel his eyes away. She gleamed, wearing a peach cold shoulder blouson top, black leather leggings, and open-toe stilettos. Her hair was bone-straight with a center part, and her makeup was fashion-model flawless.

"You look amazing," Jami took Aurora's hand as she walked down the stairs.

"Thank you." Aurora rubbed her palm across the lapel of Jami's gray sports jacket, then touched the collar of the navy and silver polka dot shirt. "You clean up quite well yourself." She glanced over her shoulder and leaned back, giving him a once-over.

"Don't be checking out my butt," he teased, covering his

rear with his hands.

"I'm admiring the fit of your jeans, Jamison——and if your butt happens to be filling them out in all the right places, then well …" she mumbled, snickering.

"I feel objectified." He opened the truck door, gesturing toward the seat. "Get your beautiful lying-self inside."

Thirty minutes later, they arrived at a brown store front. The words LSC Dance Studio and a silhouette of a couple dancing was on the picture window.

"When you said we were going dancing this isn't what I pictured."

"It'll be fun."

They took a two hour beginners salsa class with six other couples. One hour of instruction and the second hour practicing their moves. Jami was impressed how fast Aurora learned the basic and side basic steps. Her exaggerated hip action was tantalizing.

"Have you taken dance classes before?" Jami asked, holding the closed frame salsa basic with his right hand on Aurora's left shoulder blade.

"This is my first time," she replied, following Jami's lead.

"You're a natural, and you're doing it in tall, skinny heels which I think are quite sexy."

Aurora cheeks flushed pink. "Are you flirting with me?"

"I'm just making an observation," Jami commented, holding Aurora's hand above her head, guiding her into the ladies underarm turn. "You know——I'm admiring your beautiful shoes, if your feet that are attached to your long——

shapely legs just happens to be in them, then well…"

"Touché."

***

"How did you know?" Aurora inquired, her eyes sparkling. "I've always wanted to dine here."

"I didn't." He reached across the table for her hand. "I guess it was fate." Aurora placed her hand in his. "Rumor has it that they have the best live jazz band in town."

"How is it you know so much about my hometown?"

"I did a lot of research while planning this trip."

Aurora's eyes narrowed. "Was this place on your list of things to do with your wife?"

"Truthfully. No." He gazed into her eyes, applying gentle pressure to Aurora's hand for reassurance. "Tonight. This place. Our date, is all about you. I want you to know that there's more to me than playing games, and that I know how to show a gorgeous and intelligent woman, a great grown-up time."

"Well, you've succeeded. I'm so happy that we've shared this time together. Jamison, you are an amazing man, and I'm thrilled to have known you on a more personal level."

Jami softly kneaded her knuckles with his thumb, lost in the words coming from her mouth.

"It's a shame things have to end," she uttered, gently raking her fingertips across Jami's wrist. "I feel like we just got started. Maybe it's too soon to say where or if this is headed somewhere, but I feel like there's more to us than these three days."

"Me too, but if nothing else comes of this, we've begun a beautiful friendship."

"How's everyone doing out there tonight?" a man asked in a smooth baritone voice through a microphone, standing on a raised platform with instruments and musicians behind him.

Some patrons responded, and others clapped. Jami had been so enthralled with Aurora that he missed the band setting up.

"We're going to have a great time, so relax, enjoy your dinner, dance a little, and let the sounds from Forever Jazzin' Brass Band move through you." The man gestured to the band as the house lights dimmed a little more.

"Dance a little——I thought the class——." Aurora paused, giving Jami a side-way glance. "You said no more surprises."

"I told you I was taking you dancing." Jami grinned, sitting back as the waiter placed ciabatta rolls and butter on the table, then poured water in wine glasses. "I'm not responsible for how you interpreted what I said or meant."

"Don't get smart, Jamison Wilcox." She pursed her thin glossy lips, batting her lengthy eyelashes.

"Smart is the only way I know how to be, Aurora Delaney," he shot back, winking twice.

"I'll give you two a little more time to decide." The waiter cleared his throat, sliding the check pad in his black apron pocket. "I'll come back in a moment."

"My apologies," Jami said, signaling for the waiter to remain at the table. "We'll place our drink orders now."

Halfway through dinner, the band played an up-tempo jazz number that had them bouncing and swaying in their seats. Jami glanced around, seeing that they weren't the only ones feeling the vibrant shrill coming from the trumpet as patrons migrated to the dance floor.

"Feels like Mardi Gras. You know, the kind of music that you feel all the way down in your bones," Jami commented, moving his shoulders and snapping his fingers to the sonorous beat. "Let's dance."

Jami stood, taking Aurora's hand, and she followed him to the wooden parquet floor that was filling up quicker than every breath blown through the French and euphoniums horns, bass and tenor trombones, and tubas.

They danced the night away, incorporating what they learned in class. By the time, they'd finished, Jami had shed his sports jacket, unbuttoned and rolled up his shirt sleeves, and the ends of Aurora's hair were wet and plastered to her shoulders and upper back.

***

"This was one of the best nights of my life," Jami said, escorting Aurora to her front door. "I'm not ready for it to end."

"Neither am I," she replied, unlocking the door. "Come inside."

Jami inhaled a deep breath and held it. "Do you think that's a good idea?"

"It's our last night together," Aurora replied, taking him by the hand. "I want to spend as much time with you as possible before you hop on your flight in the morning, leaving me with nothing but memories. Get in here."

Jami crossed the threshold into a place he yearned to be, although he had reservations. He and Aurora hadn't been alone since the time they'd almost kissed in his cabin six days ago.

"Make yourself comfortable," Aurora said, sliding a hand along the back of the sofa. "I'll be right back."

The layout was the same as the cabin he stayed in, except everything was on the opposite side. Her place had a more personal feel with family photos, knickknacks, and updated kitchen accessories like a KitchenAid and air fryer.

Jami removed his sports jacket, then sat on the sofa. His body gelled into the cushion, relaxing him. Laying his head back, Jami closed his eyes, and inhaled. Aurora's feminine woodsy scent lingered in the sofa fabric, letting him know that this was a place where she spent most of her time.

Churning pipes, followed by a burst of whooshing water filled the air. Jami's eyes opened, immediately registering the sound. Aurora was taking a shower.

The idea of her being naked only feet away from him, made Jami overheat, and as tempting as it was to join her, he controlled himself. He shut his eyes again and let the soothing water sounds take him to a place of mental tranquility.

"Sorry about that," Aurora said, entering the living room, startling Jami. "I didn't mean to take so long. I had to change out of those sweaty clothes. Can I get you something to drink?" she asked, going into the kitchen.

"A bottle of water, please."

Jami grinned inwardly. Aurora had indeed got comfortable in a pair of loose-fitting shorts, a tank top, and fuzzy socks. She gave Jami the water, perched on the cocktail table in front of him, resting her forearms on his thighs.

"How come you haven't tried to kiss me these past several days?" Aurora asked, leaning so close that Jami could smell her minty breath. "If you're feeling anywhere close to what I'm feeling, I know you want to."

That was direct. Jami took a large gulp of water. "I didn't want to cross any boundaries," he said, drinking more water. "Last time——your reaction."

"All of that was null and void when you changed the playing field. Besides, we've gotten to know each other much better since then and have connected on another level," Aurora countered, taking the bottle from his hands, sitting it on the cocktail table, then leaning over him. Her bra-free breast swept across his chest, exposing ample cleavage.

She placed her lips on his mouth, and Jami engulfed them with vehement intensity. All of the feelings he kept under wraps broke free. He lowered Aurora onto his lap, running his fingers through her wet hair with one hand, and cupping her rear end with the other. She gave a low moan as the kiss deepened, unbuttoning Jami's shirt.

Jami lifted Aurora, carrying her across the room and laying her on top of the pool table. She arched her back as he kissed her thigh right above the knee. Hooking his fingers in the waistband of her shorts, he pulled them halfway down.

"Wait a minute." Jami inched backward.

Panting, Aurora lifted on her elbows. "What's wrong?"

"I can't do this."

Aurora wiggled her shorts off, twirling them on her foot, then flicking them to the floor in front of Jami's feet. Giggling, she jumped down, then grabbed his belt buckle.

"I can't," Jami clutched Aurora's hand, releasing a frustrating sigh. "Not like this."

"You don't want me?"

Jami rubbed his clean, but moist scalp. "Every inch of my body wants you," he groaned, staring at her bare derriere, wanting nothing more than to make his home between her legs. "But not like this. I didn't sign the papers. I'm still married, and that means something to me. I can't break the vows that I made to God, myself, or Harper, regardless of her actions."

Aurora laid her forehead against his chest.

"When and if we do ever make love, I don't want to have any regrets. I want things to be right."

"You're an honorable man. One your wife, clearly took for granted," she said in a somber tone, retrieving the shorts, and sliding her legs into them. "I guess this is goodbye."

"It doesn't have to be," Jami replied, lifting her chin. "I can extend my stay for another week."

Aurora's eyes lit up. "You'd do that for me?"

"I'll do that for us," he corrected, placing a tender kiss on her lips. "Make no mistake——I am feeling you just as much as you are me, and I'm open to wherever this may lead."

Chapter 17

Images of DaJuan played on repeat while Harper packed. If she could stay another seven days, she would … she'd settle for another twelve hours if it were possible.

Harper walked out of her room to get her toiletries from the bathroom, and ran into Michelle, who shoved her hard.

"Damn, Chelle. That hurt," Harper shouted, rotating her shoulder that crashed into the door frame.

"I didn't know you were here. Why didn't you call to let us know you were coming in?"

"I spoke with Bianca around four this morning. She let me in," Harper countered, moving into the bathroom. "I left the keycard in my other purse. I didn't want to bang on the door that early and scare the crap out of her." She unfastened a small cloth bag, then glanced at Michelle. "I thought you'd be with Eldon."

"He hung out here with us last night. Bianca made her famous margaritas, and Eldon brought ackee and saltfish. It was tasty."

Harper glanced at her watch. "Are you going to see him before you leave? We have about three hours before we have to be at the airport."

"We already said our goodbyes," Michelle said, and they both turned toward the threshold as Bianca dragged her feet into the bathroom. "Good morning sleepyhead."

"It's her fault," Bianca shot back, pointing at Harper.

"Guilty." Harper dropped the bag on the counter and held her hands up.

"Whatever, silly." Bianca shoved her aside, twisting the hot and cold-water knobs until a steady stream ran from the faucet like Niagara Falls.

"So, are you going to tell us where DaJuan took you last night?" Michelle asked while Bianca washed her face, and brushed her teeth.

"Let's just say that I'm a proud member of the mile-high club," Harper moaned, rubbing a hand across her breasts. "Having an orgasm while flying above the mountains is better than anything I could've ever imagined."

Bianca damn near choked on the toothpaste.

"You go girl." Michelle danced in a circle. "He's sending

you home *right*."

"Ohhh yesssss." Harper nodded, putting the toiletries in the bag. "I can't help but wonder am I just one of the many women that DaJuan's had a weekend fling with."

"What difference does it make? You're not trying to build something with this guy." Michelle shrugged. "You had a girl's trip with an island rendezvous you'll never forget."

"There's that, but——"

"Do you have feelings for him?" Bianca asked, staring at Harper through the mirror.

"I'd be lying if I said no."

"Harper nooooo." Bianca wiped her mouth with a face towel, then turned to look at her. "DaJuan was supposed to be a good time, that's it."

"He put it on you and you done fell in love," Michelle said, leaning against the wall with a devilish grin of approval.

"It's so much more than that, I can't explain." Harper pulled her braids over her shoulder and stroked them. "When he looks at me——I feel." She clutched her chest, and her heart was beating faster than normal. "He makes me *feel*."

Bianca laid her hands across Harper's.

"I think I may have fallen in love with him."

Silence filtered the air.

"Have you told DaJuan how you feel?" Bianca asked, concern etching her facial features.

"I'm not sure if I should. Besides, I have reservations about his authenticity. He hasn't done anything to make me question it, and when we're together, he treats me like a queen——*his queen.*"

"So far, I don't hear a problem," Michelle commented.

"Me neither."

"A little voice keeps nagging me, and I can't shake it." Harper sighed, throwing her head back. "And at the same time, I can't wait to get lost in his embrace when he comes to see me in the next hour."

***

Harper sat in DaJuan's lap on the private balcony in her suite. He caressed her hip, and she melted in his arms, committing his touch and smell to memory.

"You're rather quiet," DaJuan whispered, kissing her temple.

"I'm basking in the happiness that I feel when I'm with you. I wish I could pack you in my luggage and bring you home with me."

"If only it were that simple."

"Have you ever been to America?"

"I've been to some of the southern states——Florida, Georgia, and Texas."

"Would you visit me in Chicago?" she asked, gazing into his orbs, hoping that he says what she wants to hear.

"Yes. Definitely." He smiled, pinching her chin with the softest touch. "All I needed was an invitation."

"You have an open one to use whenever you like, hopefully that'll be sooner than later."

"Non-peak season is November to mid-December."

"That's four months from now. I don't know if I can go that long without seeing you." Harper tapped his bottom lip with her index finger. DaJuan opened his mouth, pulling it inside, and sucking the tip. "You know it's going to be cold, right?"

"You'll keep me warm," he said, shifting beneath Harper. "How close is Illinois to Wisconsin?

"They're neighboring states. Why?"

"Just curious."

She marinated on the random inquiry, and even more random response for a minute, while debating if she should ask the question that's been on her mind.

"What are you thinking? You done got quiet again."

Harper straightened, playing with DaJuan's locs. "Please don't get offended, but——have you done this before with tourists? You're a wealthy man. You can have any woman you want. Why did you zero in on me?"

DaJuan tapped Harper's knee, and she rose. Immediately, he stood, cupping her face. "You're beautiful. Never question that. I was drawn to you the moment I saw you." He pulled Harper into him and kissed her like it was their last time.

"I love you," she mumbled while their tongues mingled.

Harper waited for him to bristle, but he never did. Instead, DaJuan held her tighter.

"I love you, too."

***

Harper collected her luggage from baggage claim, feeling like she flew back to an alternate reality.

"Good to go away, and good to come home," Bianca said to Harper and Michelle.

"Always," Michelle agreed, verifying the tags on her suitcase.

"Speak for yourselves," Harper countered. "The life I left behind no longer exists." She glanced at her girlfriends. "I'm not complaining. Just stating the facts."

If you need anything, you know where to find us," Michelle said, opening her arms wide.

The three of them joined in a group hug before going their separate ways.

Harper headed to Eric's house to get the apartment keys. Her first thought was to go to the home she shared with Jami, but she wasn't ready to face the girls yet. She needed more time to ride the high from her trip before answering questions.

Pulling into the empty driveway, Harper called Eric.

"Hey bro, are you home? I'm out front and I don't see the car. I didn't know if you were parked in the garage or not."

"Welcome back, sis," he greeted in an exuberant tone. "I'm running errands with Pam. We'll be back soon. Did you forget your key?"

"No," Harper replied, getting out of the car, and walking the manicured path to the front door. "Just extending the courtesy. The last thing I need is a visual of you and Pam in a compromising position in your living room."

Eric laughed hard. "That only happened once."

"That was one time too many for me. I was never supposed to see certain parts of my sister-in-law, and now I can't get the images out of my head. So, forget what you're talking about. I'll never stick my key in your door without calling first."

"Okay." Eric snickered. "EJ stepped out earlier, but he should be back home by now."

Harper whipped around.

"What's that noise?" Eric asked.

Turning toward the sound of the roaring hip-hop music, a red drop-top Chevy Camaro pulled alongside her car.

"Your son, my nephew——oh my gosh," Harper gasped, rubbing her forehead. "And my *daughters*——just pulled into the driveway."

Chapter 18

"You don't have to keep catering to me like this," Jami commented, unwrapping the plate from the homecooked breakfast Aurora brought to his hotel this morning.

"That's the least I could do since you won't let me put you up in one of the cabins."

"Aurora."

"I know. I know," she interjected, shaking her head. "You're a man. You can handle your business. You don't want to occupy the cabin when someone else could be leasing it——blah, blah, blah, blah."

"You think you're funny," Jami commented, breaking a piece of the moist biscuit covered in gravy, and feeding it to her.

"Did you stop to think that maybe I wanted you closer to me?" she asked, holding a hand in front of her mouth while she chewed and talked. "That way, we don't have to travel back and forth to see each other."

She did have a good point.

"I'll stay at the cabin as long as you let me pay for it."

"Jamison. That's not necessary."

He hummed, putting his attention back on the delicious breakfast.

Aurora folded her arms and sat quietly, but not for too long. "Fine. Have it your way," she conceded, glaring at Jami, her cheeks flushing.

"Just like Burger King."

She reached over, grabbed a decorative pillow from the couch, and threw it at him.

***

Bile jumped into the back of Harper's throat at the sight of Danica and Kylie. The sole purpose for going to her brother's house first, was to give herself more time before dealing with the questions.

"Hey, Tee-Tee Harp," EJ shouted, tilting the seat forward to let Kylie out from the backseat. "I didn't know you were coming by."

"How're you doing, EJ?" Harper glanced around her muscular nephew in a crisp tee, denim shorts, and fresh Jordan's, her eyes landing on Danica and Kylie. "Hi, girls."

Danica came forward, hugging Harper. "Hey, Ma. How was your trip?"

The rigid embrace and the tightness in her voice was thicker than a steamy shower in a closed bathroom. At least, Danica acknowledged her.

"It was good."

Harper downplayed her happiness. She couldn't beam the way her soul really felt. The girls didn't know the ins and out of her marriage, and they most certainly didn't need to know that a man, other than their dad, made Harper feel like a newlywed on her wedding night.

Kylie rushed past them, meeting EJ at the front door.

"Hey, baby girl," Harper called out, being mindful of her tone.

"Where's dad?"

That was a question that Harper couldn't answer; not because she didn't want to, but because she didn't know. Jami might already be back. Harper hadn't spoken to him in a few days, and since she didn't pay any attention to the itinerary, she didn't know the time of his return flight. The only reason Harper knew he should be home today was because of the time he'd asked her to schedule vacation.

"You might be feeling some kind of way, but I know you heard me speak to you," Harper said, moving next to Kylie.

"Hello, mother." She pushed past EJ soon as he entered

the unlock code into the keypad, trekked through the living room, then entered the bathroom, and shut the door.

Harper glanced at Danica who shrugged. Her expression matched Kylie's actions.

"EJ, would you give us a moment?" Harper asked, trying to slow her breathing. Her heart was racing and not in a good way.

He nodded, then headed up the winding staircase. Once Harper heard a door close, she maneuvered to the bathroom door, and knocked. "Kylie, let's talk. We're going to have a family meeting."

"It's not a family meeting if all members aren't present," she shot back from the other side of the door.

Harper blew out a slow breath.

"Come on, sis," Danica said, moving in front of Harper and tapping on the door. "This is mom. Let's listen to what she has to say."

After a few seconds, the lock clicked and Kylie came into the living room. The girls sat on the sofa, and Harper claimed the love seat. As much as Harper wanted to wait for Jami, she knew that wasn't an option.

"Your dad and I," she sighed, pressing her lips together. "We need some time apart."

"What exactly does *that* mean?" Danica asked, glancing at Kylie, then back at her mom. "We already know you've rented an apartment."

Harper's mouth opened, but she couldn't bring herself to say anything.

"We've seen it," Kylie huffed, her demeanor colder than Antarctica. "It's nice enough——kind of small, but I guess it would be since it's only for you."

"Excuse me." Harper frowned. "You had no right to invade my space without talking to me first. How did you——"

"EJ showed us the day he and Uncle Eric moved your things," Danica replied. "He gave us the keys to give to you when you came home from Tennessee."

"We wanted to see where you were living since you moved out and didn't discuss anything with us," Kylie replied, scowling at Harper. "Ma," she said in a raised voice, slapping her thighs. "Just be real. I found the divorce papers."

"What divorce papers?" Danica shouted, whirling her head in Kylie's direction, bounding to her feet, her chest rising and falling faster than a torpedo.

"They were laying on the end table closest to the front door on display for anyone to see," Kylie answered, pursing her lips as tears filled her eyes. "Mom was the only one who signed them."

"Ma." Danica peered through squinted eyes, glancing at Harper. "You asked dad for a divorce?"

The hurt the girls were feeling was too much to bear. One day when they had husbands, they might understand that things aren't always as they seem.

"What's going on?" Danica asked, leaning forward.

"Sometimes people grow apart. It doesn't mean that they no longer love each other."

"Don't talk to us like we're little kids," Kylie snapped. "I helped dad plan your trip. He was the happiest I'd ever seen him. He was looking forward to whisking you away to a cabin in the woods. He was taking you hiking, and canoeing, and all the things he said you'd love to do if we lived in a warmer climate," Kylie roared, wiping the tears that left skid marks down her cheeks with the back of her hand. "That was a man in love with his wife. Not one wanting a divorce."

Harper couldn't dispute that fact. Jami didn't want the divorce. She knew he loved and cared for her, but the part about him being in love with her was questionable, although the careful planning of their trip showed otherwise. Jami didn't like any of that stuff, and for him to cater to all of the things that she loved, spoke volumes. Maybe she was wrong about everything.

"Where's dad?" Danica asked, her eyes glassy with unshed tears.

"I'm not sure."

"Weren't you with him in Tennessee?" Kylie inquired, her voice peaking several notches.

"No," Harper admitted, wishing she had control of the narrative. "I was in Jamaica with Bianca and Michelle."

"You ghosted dad on your anniversary to go on a trip with your friends." Danica gasped, clutching the sofa cushion. "That's messed up."

Kylie stood, rolling her eyes heavenward, marching to the front door. "I'm out of here. The keys to your *new home* are at *our* house on the kitchen counter next to the fruit bowl."

Danica looked at her mother with disappointment, then

turned her back to Harper. "Wait up, sis. I'll join you."

The door slammed, and Harper fell back in the loveseat. She had not anticipated the reactions she received. If she had the chance to talk to the girls as opposed to them finding out things on their own, the news might had gone over smoother. Now, Harper wasn't sure what to do.

Grabbing her phone, she dialed Jami. Soon as he answered, she asked, "Where are you?" she snapped as soon as he answered.

"Excuse me?"

"Look." She paused, taking a deep breath. "I didn't mean to be so rude. I——I just talked with the girls and they didn't take the news well."

"I thought we agreed to do that together."

"They didn't leave me much choice. Kylie found the divorce papers and confronted me. I couldn't put it off."

Jami sighed, growing silent for a few seconds. "Where are they now?"

"They left, but shouldn't be too far," Harper explained, bouncing her knee. "They're on foot. I'm at Eric's house and the girls rode over here with EJ. I came here straight from the airport. Coincidentally, we arrived at the same time."

"Them leaving is probably for the best. A walk will give them some time to process things."

"I'm sure you're right. I just didn't expect——"

"You ready, Jamison?" a woman asked in the background.

Harper's knee stopped moving, and she sat upright. "Who's that?"

"I didn't know you were on the phone," the woman said. "But that's fine. I need to run over to my place and grab something. Just call me when you're done."

"Will do."

Harper fumed. The airiness of the two simple words were a stark difference from the tone of voice that Jami just spoke to her in.

"Who is that?"

He exhaled into the receiver. "You no longer get to do that."

"What?"

"Question me."

"You're my husband. I have a right to——." Harper bit her bottom lip, absorbing the words coming out of her mouth.

"Legally yes, but that's only because I didn't sign the papers. You can't have it both ways. You no longer want me, but you still want the ins and outs of my life. I've had time to think about some things of my own, and maybe——"

"You're right. I'm sorry," Harper countered, even though she still wanted to know who the woman was that spoke with ease and familiarity to her husband. "We'll talk when you get home, or are you already back?"

"Actually, I'm staying another week," Jami said, making a mental note to call his mother and let her know, so she wouldn't be worried.

"Why?" Harper asked, growing angrier and more jealous by the second. "Does it have anything to do with that woman I heard talking to you?"

Jami didn't say a word.

"Don't ignore me." Harper scooted to the edge of the loveseat, burning a hole through the hardwood floors. "I know you heard me."

"I'll see you next week."

Chapter 19

Jami drew a sharp breath, dropping his head in his hands. He knew from the moment Harper served him the divorce papers that the girls wouldn't take the news well. Now, it had bit Harper in the ass, and he was left to make things better. Not that anything he could say would ever make them splitting up all right.

Aurora tapped on the front door, peeking inside. "Is everything okay?"

Clutching the phone in his left hand, Jami waved her in, sliding over on the sofa creating room for Aurora to sit. "Not really. My daughters found the divorce papers before we had a chance to speak with them, and Kylie blew up at Harper. They stormed out upset."

Aurora sighed, laying her head on his shoulder. "Divorce is never easy, regardless of the circumstances. It's even more compounded when children are involved——even the grown ones."

"I'm sorry to keep dumping my mess on you."

"That's the least of your worries," she reassured, sliding her arm in his. "I like being here for you."

Jami laid his head on top of hers. "I like being with you. Period." He placed a kiss on her forehead, then righted himself. "But I need to call Kylie before we get going and make sure my baby girl is okay."

"Take all the time you need."

Before Aurora could stand, Jami's phone rang. Danica's picture appeared on the home screen.

"I'ma go," Aurora whispered.

Jami placed a hand on her knee. "You don't have to." He leaned forward, answering the call. "Hi, Danica."

"Dad." She sniffled. "I need to tell you something."

"Before you continue. I've already spoken to your mom, and she told me what happened," he said, his heart aching from the pain of hearing his daughter's sadness. "Where are you?"

"No," Kylie interjected out of nowhere. Danica must have Jami on speakerphone. "Where are you? Your flight was scheduled to come back this morning at ten, and we already know mom didn't go to Tennessee with you," Kylie gasped. "My gosh. Every time I talked to you, you pretended like she was right there, and the whole time she was living it up in Jamaica with her friends. What's wrong with you? You both lied to us."

Jami couldn't dispute that.

"I'm still in Tennessee. I'll be back next Friday," Jami replied, glancing at Aurora, and a smile tugged at the corners of his mouth. "Now, answer my question. Where are you?"

"Uncle Eric's house," Danica responded. "We waited for mom to leave, then came back."

"Okay." He nodded, relieved that they had returned and were safe.

"I know stepping away was probably for the best, but be mindful how you do things. The homes are gorgeous, and the people on Eric's block have been there for thirty plus years, but the surrounding area is too sketchy for you to be wandering around on foot," Jami warned.

"Why don't you sound surprised?" Kylie inquired, ignoring Jami's advice. "Did you already know that mom filed for a divorce?"

He swallowed past the lump in his throat, recalling the morning of their anniversary. Pure joy turned into sour grapes in a matter of minutes.

"Yes."

"When were you going to tell us?" Kylie asked. "Or doesn't our input matter?"

Jami tightly curled his toes, and took several deep breaths. "We were going to talk to you when we got home."

"Come on, dad——you know what I mean," Kylie shot

back, making him feel like he was being scolded.

He understood her reaction. Jami couldn't bring himself to tell them that he was just as shocked as they were, and that their mother orchestrated things on her own.

"The details are between me and your mom."

"Did you have me help you go all out on this getaway as a last ditch effort to save your marriage?" Kylie drilled, and Jami could hear the heaviness in her voice. "Were you holding out for hope since you didn't sign the papers?"

Jami slumped into the cushion, and Aurora stroked a gentle hand along his arm. He found comfort in her gentle touch.

"It wasn't like that, baby girl." Jami squeezed his toes even tighter, fighting the emotion that strained to break free. "That's all I'm able to say."

"You're not any more forthcoming than mom," Danica weighed in, huffing.

"It's not my intent to be difficult. The spousal relationship is different from the parental one, even though one effects the other, our marital business is between us," Jami explained, rubbing his forehead. "I know that's not what y'all want to hear, but I hope you understand."

No words were spoken as silence was traded for anymore debate, and Jami wondered what the girls were thinking.

"I need more time to process this," Kylie finally retorted, her voice soft and dejected. "No one wants to hear that their parents are getting divorced, especially when the reasons aren't clear. I have to go——I'll talk to you later."

"Bye, dad," Danica said, and the call ended.

"Damn." Jami stood, and walked into the kitchen, placing the phone on the barstool. Gripping the edge of the counter, he lunged forward with his head hanging between his arms.

"What's wrong?" Aurora asked, rushing to his side.

"I hate lying to my girls." Jami frowned, turning around, swiping his phone, and claiming the barstool seat. "A lie of omission is still a lie. I can't tell them the truth, and throw Harper under the bus, even though she belongs there. She's still their mother."

"You're a good man, Jamison Wilcox, and an even better father. Don't look at it as a lie. What you did was selfless, putting Kylie and Danica's feelings first."

Aurora moved in front of Jami, wrapping her arms around his waist. He returned her embrace, and held onto her until he felt better.

"Thanks for being you." He lifted Aurora until her feet were off the ground, burying his head in her curls. "You're an amazing woman."

***

The next several days, Jami checked in with the girls every morning and every evening. He encouraged them to speak with their mother, reenforcing that the dissolution of the marriage had nothing to do with the relationship they had with their mother. Danica was more receptive than Kylie. He had ended the call with Kylie, when Aurora walked onto the back deck covered in an oversized beach towel, and seemingly nothing else.

"Are you trying to seduce me, woman?" Jami asked, sitting in the wooden rocking chair with a beer in his hand.

"I'd love too, however …" Aurora sauntered by, relieved Jami of his beer, took a swig, then handed the cold bottle back to him. "I respect your moral compass."

Why do I have to be a stand-up guy, cause I swear, I'd love nothing more than to be sandwiched between her and that towel.

"I thought we were going out this evening," Jami said, his eyes fixed on Aurora's silky legs.

"Let's see," she hummed, positioning herself in front of him, clutching the towel. "We've been out every night this week." She lifted four fingers, and counted. "Karaoke, wine tasting, miniature golf, and bowling. And, I'm not even sure if I can count bowling because you filled in for one of the guys whose wife went into labor."

Jami smiled, still drinking in the addictive body of vivaciousness that stood before him.

"I'm going to take care of you tonight." Aurora dropped the towel, revealing the skimpiest bikini he'd ever seen.

"Mmmm. Mmmm. Mmmm." Jami bit his bottom lip, crossing his legs and folding his hands while positioning the beer bottle over his midsection, praying it camouflaged the hard-on that sprung to life.

The strapless bikini top had a large middle-opening, exposing most of her full breasts, and the bottom had a tiny triangular piece of fabric, just enough to cover her private area, held together by a G-string, showing off Aurora's peach-shaped rear. Jami had gone to heaven in hopes of being reincarnated as himself, so he could have this exact moment all over again.

"We're finally going to utilize this hot tub," Aurora said, sashaying to the other side of the deck, and removing the protective cover. Jami rushed over to assist. "Change into your trunks." She perched on the side, turning the knobs until the water flowed. "I'll be waiting."

Jami changed in record time. He continued to tell himself to behave, and not to let his hormones take control of his mind. When he stepped onto the deck, Aurora was already shoulder deep under the rumbling water with her hair pinned in a messy bun. Jami climbed in opposite of Aurora, and the heated water felt amazing on his muscles.

"I don't know why you're all the way over there," she teased, resting a foot on his stomach. "Come over here."

Against Jami's better judgement, he obliged. "Okay—now what?" he asked as the water swished from his movement.

"Turn around, and lay back," she said, positioning her legs along the sides of the tub.

Jami rested his back against her breasts, and Aurora placed her legs around his waist, letting them fall freely over his thighs. The softness of her body and the massaging jets were enough to soothe him.

Aurora kneaded his back, shoulders, and upper arms. Laying his forearms along her legs, Jami inhaled, breathing in the steam that lifted from the water.

"Your hands are magical."

She walked her fingertips up his neck, applying gentle pressure behind his ears with her thumbs, while massaging his temples at the same time with her index and middle fingers.

Jami couldn't remember the last time Harper had touched him like this ... deliberate and intimate.

"You deserve to feel good, too," Aurora whispered as if reading his thoughts. Then she slid firm hands under his armpits until they landed on his robust chest, causing a moan to escape Jami's mouth.

"This feels so incredible," Jami uttered, scooting down further and laying his head back on Aurora's shoulder. The tension, and the days of worrying, seeped from his mind and spirit with every stroke, rub, and manipulative pressed finger on his body.

The bubbling water, soft wind, and the insects singing in the woods was the perfect soundtrack to their evening. Jami closed his eyes, and drifted into the most restful sleep he'd had in days.

"Jamison. Hey. Wake up."

He felt Aurora tapping his shoulder. Awaking, he immediately noticed the change in the air. The wind bit more crisp on his wet body, and the water temperature was lukewarm, if that.

Shivering, he asked, "How long have I been sleep?"

"Five minutes longer than me," she replied, wrapping her arms around him.

Jami lifted her fingers, and kissed them. "Let's go inside." He stood, helping Aurora to her feet, then grabbing her beach towel, and enclosing her inside of it.

He ushered her in the cabin, and Jami closed and locked the sliding patio door. When he turned around to head to the bathroom for a towel, Aurora started drying him off with hers.

"That's sweet of you." Jami's heart melted as she dried his legs, but his happiness faded when he heard Aurora's teeth chattering, and by the time she reached his stomach, her lips were quivering. "Oh no." He rushed her over to the bed, yanking the quilt back. She laid down and Jami pulled the soft covering up to her neck.

"You need to get under here too before you get sick," Aurora suggested, flipping the quilt back on the other side of the bed.

"I'll be fine," Jami backed away. "All I need to do is change out of these wet trunks."

He snatched a pair of shorts from the suitcase nearby, then disappeared into the bathroom. When he reemerged, Aurora still had the covering pulled back.

"I'm going to turn on the heat, and use the throw blanket on the sofa," Jami said, backpedaling toward the living room.

"Jamison," Aurora called out in a sensual tone that halted his movement. "I want to lay in your arms. I want *you,* to keep me warm."

Exhaling, he whispered, "You know where I stand."

"No sex," she commented in a soft voice. "Just you, and your body next to mine. That's it. I promise."

He stood there for a moment, thinking of all the ways things could go wrong.

"Jamison."

Blinking, he moved to the same suitcase, plucking two t-shirts out, handing one to Aurora. She sat upright, sliding her head and arms into the shirt, then untied the bikini top, and pulled the minute piece of sexy fabric out from the shirt sleeve.

Jami was familiar with that move. He'd seen Harper remove a bra like that in less than five seconds without exposing herself many times. He put on his t-shirt, approaching the opposite side of the bed, glancing at the beautiful woman waiting for him to join her. As soon as he laid down, Aurora pulled the quilt over Jami, lifted the remote from the bedside table, then scooted close to him.

He released uneasy laughter, moving backward. "You need to lie under the sheet and I'll stay on top of it," Jami warned, as she adjusted the bedding, her G-string bikini bottom had Aurora's rear on full display until she tugged the shirt down. "That's the only way this is going to work."

They cuddled in a spooned position, attempting to watch a movie on cable, but instead, the movie watched them sleep. That was until the ringing phone that Jami swore he heard in his dreams, awakened him.

Jami yawned, trying to rise when he realized that Aurora's limbs were draped over him as if he were a human body pillow. He gently slid to the side, so he wouldn't wake her, almost falling out of the bed.

The ringing stopped. Jami stretched, and was about to get back in the bed when the phone rang again. As he trekked from the bedroom into the living room, beaming sunlight shone through the slit in the curtains. At that moment, he realized that they had spent their first night together.

"Hello," Jami groaned, answering the call, not bothering to see whose name was on the screen.

"Daddy, Kylie needs you," Danica said in an alarming tone.

"What's happened?"

"She's completely shut off. She won't talk to me or mom, and——Kylie's just not herself."

"She sounded okay when I spoke with her last night," Jami countered, peering through the slit, relishing the stillness of the morning.

"That's the façade she puts on for you. I think Kylie's depressed. She even mentioned taking off a year, and not applying for the residency program."

Jami's heart sank to the floor. "That can't happen. She loves dentistry, and that's all she ever wanted to become."

"Exactly," Danica commented, releasing a quiet sigh. "I'll be the first to admit that I was caught off guard when I learned of the divorce, but after a few days to marinate on things, I've accepted it," she said, her tone a bit derisive. "I don't like it, and there are a lot of unanswered questions, but it is what it is. Kylie's not there yet. Far from it."

Jami took a deep breath, processing all that Danica said, and the things she didn't say pertaining to her own feelings.

"I'm so glad you told me. I'll be on the first flight home. In the meantime, keep an eye on your sister."

"I will."

"And remember, I'm here for you, too. You can share how you feel even if you think I don't want to hear it."

After a slight pause, Danica replied, "I know, daddy, but right now, Kylie needs you more."

"See you soon."

Chapter 20

The past four days had been hell for Harper. Not only did she have to deal with the reality that Jami stayed in Tennessee with some woman, but Kylie still refused to talk with her. That didn't stop Harper from trying though. In the interim, she focused her energy on making her apartment a home.

After unpacking the last box, Harper poured herself a glass of wine, then sunk into the furry, plush champagne-colored bean bag chair in the bedroom. "Alexa, play the Kem playlist," Harper called out to the smart speaker sitting on the corner wall shelf.

Kem's mellow voice crooned over the smooth jazz instruments, creating the perfect melody while she scrolled social media on her phone. Harper was typing in DaJuan's name to see if he had a profile when the stuttering facetime alert rang.

Grinning she answered, "Your timing couldn't have been better. I was just thinking about you, now I get to see your face."

"Hey, beautiful." DaJuan smiled wide. "You got a whole vibe going," he said, swaying and snapping his fingers.

Harper lifted her glass. "I finally finished unpacking."

"That's cause enough to celebrate."

"Agreed." She took a sip of the red wine. "Now, if my daughters would just give me a chance to explain …"

Squinting, DaJuan asked, "What's going on there? Your entire mood shifted before my eyes."

"I'm——not," she mumbled, shaking her head. "I had to talk to my daughters about me and their father before I was ready, and they didn't take it well. On top of that, I called Jami to tell him what's going on, and he … never mind. It's nothing."

"It's absolutely *something* if you're this upset," DaJuan countered in his soothing accented tone. "You know you can talk to me."

"Alexa, turn the music off," Harper ordered, taking another sip of the wine. "I feel like such a hypocrite. How dare Jami claim to love me and want our marriage to work, and he's in Tennessee, the place he was taking, *me,* for our anniversary, with some woman," she vented, not able to look DaJuan in the eyes. "Why is this bothering me so much? I'm the one who asked for the divorce."

"It's okay to have second thoughts."

Harper didn't expect DaJuan to say that.

"You've been with the man your entire adult life. It would be a little remiss if you claimed to feel nothing for him."

"Aren't you understanding?"

"Life happens to all of us …" DaJuan replied, his voice trailing off.

"What does that mean?"

"We all want something that's a little out of reach, for one reason or another. Reality is sobering. It makes you reevaluate your choices," DaJuan explained, looking at Harper. "I take nothing away from our time together. We had a fantasy three-day romance, and it was beautiful. I loved every minute of it, and we've developed feelings for each other, but at the same time, this is not your reality," DaJuan said. "You have a whole life that you went home to with a husband and two daughters who love you."

"I thought you said you loved me," Harper commented, finally giving DaJuan direct eye contact.

He moved the phone closer to his face. "I do. That's why I want what's best for you. If staying with your husband is it, then who am I to stand in the way of that."

Harper remained silent.

DaJuan blew out a long breath which made Harper anxious. "From everything you've told me about your husband——it seems like he's doing all the right things. He's taking care of you and your daughters. It appears the only thing he's guilty of is working too much." DaJuan's background switched from sunny outdoors to off-white walls and complete silence. "All men are guilty of that, at least the ones are who take care of their families or have businesses to run."

"So, what are you saying?"

"Never mistake what you mean to me. I haven't felt this kind of connection with anyone ever. And I know, me speaking on your husband's behalf doesn't work in my favor, but I'm just saying it bears rethinking."

Before Harper could speak a rebuttal, Jami's face appeared on the phone screen. "Look who we've spoken up. I'll give you a call back."

"Bye, beautiful."

Harper clenched her teeth, then tapped the green button. "I'm surprised to be hearing from you," she answered not masking her contempt.

"I'm going to overlook the sarcasm in your voice and focus on the reason for my call," Jami remarked, clearing his throat. "I spoke with Danica and she said that Kylie is having a hard time with what's going on between us."

"I'm aware," Harper replied, carefully setting the wine glass on the carpet. "I get updates from Danica because Kylie refuses to answer my calls. I even went by the house, figuring she'd have to acknowledge my presence if I'm in her face, but that just made it worse."

"At least you're seeing how she really feels," Jami shot back, in a concerned tone. "I talk to her twice a day, and she gives me the impression that everything's okay."

"I don't know what to do," Harper admitted, glancing at Kylie's framed graduation picture she placed on the dresser earlier. "You said that they wouldn't take it well, but I didn't foresee this. I feel like we broke the news to a pair of pre-teens, and not twenty-somethings. What do we do?"

"Don't do anything until I get there. My flight lands at four-twenty."

"I thought——"

"Come by the house. I should be there by five-thirty——six at the latest," Jami interjected. "Kylie needs both of us."

***

"I hate that I have to leave like this," Jami said, removing his suitcase from Aurora's pickup truck in the departure lanes at McGhee Tyson Airport. "I've loved every second of every minute of every hour we've shared together." He closed the door, then pulled Aurora into his arms. "I miss you already."

"Keep it moving. Let's go." The male traffic aide waved them along, wearing a neon orange vest with yellow reflectors.

"I feel the same," she whispered, holding onto Jami, sliding a hand in his back pants pocket. "I have a secret——I kept your t-shirt as a reminder of the night we officially slept together. It smells like you."

"You can have anything you want."

Aurora raised an eyebrow and gave him a lopsided grin.

"Except that." Jami ran his fingers through her hair. "At

least, not yet."

"Let's go. Let's go," the stocky man ordered, coming their way.

Aurora lifted on her tiptoes, planting a kiss on Jami's lips. She placed a finger in the center of his chest. "You owe me three more days. I don't care when, or where, just make sure I get my full weeks' time."

"That can be arranged."

"All right now." The traffic aide fussed, speaking into a radio. "This was your last warning."

"Goodbye, Jamison." Aurora waved, dashing around to the driver's side, then shouted, "don't forget to check your back pocket."

"What?" He patted his buttocks.

Aurora blew him a kiss, hopped in the truck, then pulled off as a yellow tow truck headed her way.

Jami checked his luggage with the Skycap, then proceeded to the security checkpoint, pulling a folded beige piece of paper from his pocket.

A check for seven hundred dollars was enclosed. "Aurora," he said under his breath as he read the note.

I know if I tried to give you any amount of money back, you'd refuse it. I wanted you here, and there's no price tag on us spending time with each other. So, I gave you half. That's fair, and I don't have to hear you schooling me on what it is that a man does. You have that in spades. Until next time, Aurora

xoxo

Chapter 21

"If someone would've told me I'd be apprehensive seeing my husband after eleven days apart, I wouldn't believe them," Harper said to Bianca who was on the car speakerphone. "Sometimes, weeks and months would go by with Jami being on the road, but this time is different."

"It would be. So much has changed," Bianca commented. "Nevertheless, I still don't understand why you're sitting in the car and aren't in the house with your girls."

"I don't feel comfortable just walking in. It's no longer my home."

"Then ring the damn bell," Bianca advised, her bossy tone

falling between being Harper's best friend and mother. "That will always be your home. You and Jami raised a family there for over twenty-some odd years. Stop being foolish. He didn't put you out. You left on your own accord."

"Way to kick your best friend when she's down," Harper whined, checking the time. "I wouldn't expect this from you."

"I'm going to let that one slide," Bianca replied, huffing. "I'm only keeping you honest. You know I love you enough to tell you the truth."

"Maybe I don't want to hear it."

After a slight pause, Bianca asked, "Are you having second thoughts?"

"I'm not sure what I'm having," Harper admitted, resting her hands in her lap. "I fell in love with DaJuan hard and fast. Last week was magical, and I've felt more alive than ever. He had the nerve to tell me I should rethink things with Jami. What do you think about that?"

"I think he may be right, but it's not up to me. What do *you* feel?"

Harper released a slow breath. "I don't know." She glanced down at her left ring finger where her wedding band used to be. "I love Jami, but I'm tired of us barely coexisting. I'm alone most of the time, and I can be alone by myself."

"But is that what you really want? That man loves you. He's out there busting his butt to make sure you don't want for anything. You know I know what's up because my husband's out there with him."

"Yeah, but Trevor is home way more often than Jami,"

Harper remarked.

"True. However, we're not putting two girls through college and grad school either."

Harper glanced into the rearview mirror, and her heart raced. "Jami's here. I'll talk to you later." She ended the call, and took a deep breath.

He stepped out of the truck, and her racing heart skipped several beats. Jami looked good, well rested, and tanned. That Morris Chestnut swagger was in full gear. Harper wrung her hands as he approached the passenger's side, then opened the door.

"Hey." He gave Harper a half smile. "Is it all right if I sit?"

"Of course." She moved her purse from the seat, and placed it on the middle console. "Thanks for coming back sooner than planned. I appreciate it."

"Anything for my girls."

Harper used to be part of that equation, but she was certain that he only meant the two girls he helped create.

Jami narrowed his gaze on her. "Why are you sitting out here?"

"Waiting for you. I couldn't face them alone."

He shifted, angling toward Harper. "Honestly, I'm glad you did. I want to talk with you first, so we have a clear understanding of where we stand before speaking with them."

She nodded, searching his eyes. Harper didn't know what he was thinking, and that worried her.

"When you sprung the divorce on me, I was devastated. It felt like you gripped my heart with your bare hands and ripped it from my chest," Jami said in a meek voice. "I didn't understand. I didn't know why. I played that morning over and over again in my head, trying to figure out what I did wrong, and if I could make things better."

"Jami." Harper touched his hand, but he pulled away.

"Let me finish." He exhaled so hard that his nostrils flared.

"Just wait a minute." Harper laid her hand over his. Jami was trembling. "I never meant to hurt you."

"But you did." Jami shook his hand until she moved hers. She didn't try to stop him. "If you were feeling unloved and undesired——that's a conversation. You filed *papers*. You took the time to consult an attorney *behind my back*. That's not cool. Then you planned a trip, *behind my back,* disregarding my feelings. I begged for extra routes, and worked through my normal time off to accumulate four weeks of vacation to spend time with you, and for what? Then you go and rent an apartment, again, *behind my back*. That doesn't happen overnight. While I'm out earning a living for all of us, you were out securing a future without me. Why didn't you talk to me first if you were *that* unhappy?"

Reflecting on DaJuan and Bianca's words, Harper considered giving the marriage another chance. Even though she loved DaJuan and looked forward to seeing him in four months, the probability of that happening was slim, and a long distance relationship was something she refused to sign up for. That would be worse than her current situation with her husband.

"I didn't know how to tell you all that I was feeling,"

Harper admitted, lowering her gaze. After a few seconds, she looked Jami square in the eyes and hoped he heard her plea for grace and mercy. "But I think with some changes, we can give our marriage another try. I'm willing——are you?"

"It's too late," Jami said, holding praying hands under his chin. "I can't trust you."

"You can't forgive me."

"I'm saying, I can't trust you," Jami reiterated, closing his eyes for a quick second. "I can forgive most anything. We're human. We make mistakes. I'm saying, I can't trust that the next time you're upset or feeling slighted, that you won't make life-altering decisions behind my back. You divorced me, moved out of our home, and traveled out of the country, Harper," Jami's voice hitched. "I love you, but I can't go through that again. I won't."

Harper sat quietly, absorbing his words.

"Who is she?" Harper asked, twiddling her thumbs.

"Her name is Aurora," Jami said, and Harper swore she saw a hint of a smile when he mentioned her name. "But she has nothing to do with my decision."

"I find that hard to believe," Harper whispered, looking out of the window. "Do you love her? Is she worth throwing our marriage away?"

"Please don't," Jami snapped, folding his arms across his chest. "You put this entire thing in motion. For all I know, you had a boy toy waiting for you down in Jamaica. Is that another thing you planned *behind my back*?"

"You know me better than that."

"Do I?" Jami asked, leaning all the way forward until Harper turned around and faced him. "Did you spend time with someone in Jamaica?"

Harper sighed, thinking about DaJuan and how much joy he brought to her life in such a short period. She wasn't ashamed of him and at the time, he was exactly what Harper needed.

"I did. His name's DaJuan," Harper confessed, watching Jami's facial expression change. She still couldn't read it though.

"Did you sleep with him?"

Harper shifted in the seat, then glanced at Jami. "Yes."

"Mmmm hmmm." Jami rocked back and forth, rubbing the palm of his hands on his thighs.

This was the first time Harper could gauge Jami's feelings.

"So, you're an adulterer, too," he accused, his voice laced with anger.

"You have no right to judge me," Harper shot back, pointing a finger at him. "You planned to stay an additional week down there with Aurora, so don't call me any names when you've done the same."

"I didn't sleep with her," Jami shouted, hitting the dashboard. "Out of respect for our marriage, I refrained, regardless how much I may have wanted to."

"Yeah. Right."

"What reason do I have to lie?" Jami yelled, giving Harper a side-eyed glance. "You left me, remember? No one would blame me if I did——but I didn't."

Gripping the steering wheel, Harper clenched her teeth. "And you never answered my question. Do you love her?"

"I call you out, and you want to deflect, but that's okay," Jami snickered, shaking his head.

"I have strong feelings for her, but I can't say if it's love yet. But I do want to see where it leads."

"Do you love him?" Jami asked, his brows knitting together.

An image of her and DaJuan's escapades in the tent at the Blue Mountains in Saint Thomas flashed before her eyes, causing her to automatically smile. "I didn't plan to, but I do."

They sat in complete silence for five minutes, leaving Harper alone with her feelings while wondering what Jami was thinking.

"So, this is it," Jami whispered, steepling his fingers under his chin. "We've built a beautiful life together. However, it's time for our chapter as husband and wife to close." He glanced at Harper with an expression she couldn't quite read. "Part of me will always love you. I don't approve of your method or what you did——but I'm okay with things."

Harper didn't need his approval, but it was good to know they were on the same page.

"I will always love you." She angled her body toward him. "We will forever be family."

"Eternally." Jami nodded, exchanging a glance with Harper. "You all right?"

"I am," she drew a sharp breath, looking into Jami's eyes, and finding peace. "I'm ready to face the girls."

"We'll do it together."

About The Author

National Bestselling Author, **London St. Charles** has always had a passion for the pen, paper, and books. She is a Chicago native who uses the Windy City as a backdrop to the contemporary women's fiction, crime fiction, interracial romance, and romantic suspense stories she writes. London has contributed to three anthologies, *Sugar*, *Just One Kiss*, and *Evanescence*, one series, *Kings of the Castle,* with New York Times and USA TODAY Bestselling authors. Her debut novel, *The Husband We Share*, hit the AALBC Bestsellers List within six months of release and was followed by her recent literary offerings: *Betrayal of Trust, King of Chatham, Sugarcoated Deception, Deadly Deception, and Under the Tree.* She has five more projects in the pipeline for 2021. She is a beta reader, manuscript evaluator, and a proud member of several writer's groups.

FOLLOW LONDON ON SOCIAL MEDIA

Amazon Author Page: https://bit.ly/amazonauthorpagelsc

Facebook Author Page: https://bit.ly/fbauthorpagelsc

Goodreads: https://bit.ly/goodreadslsc

BookBub: https://bit.ly/bookbublsc

Instagram: https://bit.ly/instagramlsc

Twitter: https://bit.ly/twitterlsc

London Writes Newsletter: https://bit.ly/londonwritesnewsletter

Website: www.londonstcharles.com

Chasing the Unexpected: Harper and DaJuan's Story
(Unexpected Series Book 2)

Harper Wilcox now goes by Harper Moore since her divorce from Jami. She's adjusting to single life and learning that things aren't always what they seem. Her heart is longing for DaJuan, and she's counting down the days until he's able to visit. Four months seems like an eternity, but Harper's in for a surprise when DaJuan shows up in the States two months earlier than expected. Will their Jamaican romance pick up where it left off?

Coming Summer/Fall 2021

Claiming the Unexpected: Jami and Aurora's Story
(Unexpected Series Book 3)

Jami's back on the road, enjoying his new release on life. The once dreaded long hauls through the southern states, has turned into a pleasant affair now that Jami gets to see Aurora on a regular basis. What started out as a friendship brought on from unforeseen events has blossomed into a romance that continues to get better over time.

Coming Winter 2021

The Husband We Share

Xavier Carter is leading the ultimate double life. He is married to not one, but two beautiful, intelligent, professional women. Over the years, he has taken extreme measures to keep both homes happy—and separate.

Patricia, the first Mrs. Carter, believes that Xavier has left his playboy ways in the past. She had been warned to stay away from the "Campus Casanova," but didn't listen. Now she's finding that something's not quite right in their world. Unfortunately, Patricia can't focus on him when she has a secret of her own that has shadowed her since age sixteen. Fate has been unkind in the fact that her "secret" is actually watching her every move, waiting for the chance to destroy Patricia and her family.

Lauren, the second Mrs. Carter, is an independent, down to earth, home girl from New York with enough passion and sassiness to keep her husband intrigued, and the presence of mind not to be taken for a ride. She gave Xavier an ultimatum and Mr. Carter managed to put a ring on it, even though, unknown to her, he'd already made a lifetime commitment to his college sweetheart.

Shawn Johnston has a unique and intricate connection to both "wives" and the husband, which only stirs an already complicated pot. She survived, by coming out on the opposite end of a turbulent past within the foster care system. Her quest for the one thing she craved more than anything, may cause everyone's worlds to collapse and send someone to an early grave.

All in all, when the skeletons come creaking out of the closet, two of the women will wonder if the man they share is worth dying for.

Available on Amazon

Betrayal of Trust

What do you do when you've committed a heinous crime? You run and never look back.

At least, that's what Uwezo Omari and his mother planned when they fled their hometown of Reno, Nevada and planted roots in the Midwest, far away from their tumultuous past. Or so they thought.

Fifteen years later, Uwezo, now known as Chef Cedrick Dalton, is a loving husband, father, and successful businessman. Still haunted by the sins from his childhood, he treads carefully by keeping a low profile. Unfortunately, having a booming restaurant in an affluent neighborhood, the anonymity that he once coveted is now a thing of the past.

With the anniversary of the worst day of his life nearing, Cedrick's feelings of guilt and paranoia are triggered and kick into high gear. The mysterious phone calls and anonymous notes stating that someone is looking for him doesn't help. The belief that his mind is playing tricks on him vanishes when he runs into Victoria, his childhood friend who knows his secret. Turmoil is brewing because Cedrick's wife, Sierra, is unaware of his past and Victoria now threatens his freedom and puts the people he loves in danger.

Cedrick is left with life-altering decisions: tell Sierra and jeopardize her safety, or risk losing her because of this betrayal of trust? Or does he take his secret to the grave?

All options have dire consequences.

Available on Amazon

King of Chatham

Mariano "Reno" DeLuca uses his skills and resources to create safe havens for women who find themselves in dangerous situations. Unfortunately, a surge in criminal activity in the Chatham area threatens the women's anonymity and security, including the mysterious beauty who landed on the doorstep of The Second Chance at Life Women's Shelter right before an all hands on deck call that summons him to The Castle.

When Zuri Okusanya, an exotic Tanzanian Princess, arrives seeking refuge from an arranged marriage and its deadly consequences, Mariano is now forced to relocate the women in the shelter to an even more secluded place. He is striving hard not to lose his heart to the forbidden goddess, all while fighting an enemy who's supposed to be an ally and fending off immoral attempts by men who covet his seat on The Castle's board.

Will Mariano have the power to defeat his adversaries before they destroy him and the woman he loves?

Available on Amazon, Apple Books, Kobo, and Barnes and Noble

Under the Tree: Reno and Zuri's First Christmas

Zuri promises Reno that she's going to make love to him under the tree at the stroke of midnight, celebrating their first Christmas as husband and wife, and he is looking forward to that special gift. Especially since this will be the first time, he sees his wife, who's been away for three months on a business trip. But when an unexpected snowstorm keeps Zuri from catching her flight home, Reno finds himself scrambling to find a way to make it to her before midnight.

Will Reno and Zuri reunite in time for their Christmas rendezvous under the tree?

Available on Amazon

Sugarcoated Deception (Deception Series Book 1)

Walking a tightrope of a career, a husband, and fulfilling a life-long dream is never easy. Balancing a lie, a child out of wedlock, and public scandal is almost unforgivable.

Cadence Goldsmith, a young, successful automotive engineer for a European car manufacturer, learns in the middle of an awards ceremony, that her husband fathered a child with a woman he claims to have stopped seeing long before he married Cadence.

Weighing her options, she's paralyzed by the tug of war between present life and future possibilities. She must either have blind faith in her husband and trust him when he swears he hasn't touched the other woman in seven years or cut her loses. Not willing to simply walk away, she works to uncover the sinister plans of a woman who is out to destroy them. Cadence is now racing the clock to save her marriage ... and herself.

Available on Amazon

Deadly Deception (Deception Series Book 2)

Four years have passed, and Cadence Goldsmith's family is in just as much danger as it was before they moved to Germany. Lester, the man of many evils, has still managed to evade capture for Braelyn's murder, and the trial of rogue Detective O'Brien, who had threatened Cadence, is less than one week away. She wouldn't be so worried if she weren't seven months pregnant, on top of being the star witness for the prosecution, which means Cadence has to leave the place where she feels most safe and return to Chicago and face the menaces that prey on her demise.

Cadence's husband, Jackson Goldsmith, is not on board with his wife testifying. Not only is their safety at stake, but the welfare of their daughter, Jackie, whom, through years of therapy, overcame the nightmare that Lester inflicted on her young life. Jackson's holding onto the promise that the trial will be over in enough time for them to return to Germany before the baby's born. Though Jackson feels strongly about staying put, he supports Cadence's decision and vows to protect her at all costs.

Less than twelve hours after arriving in Chicago, their greatest fears become a reality. Havoc and unforeseen coincidences consume their life, starting with vandalism to the family home. No longer knowing who she can and can't trust in law enforcement, Cadence questions every day if she made the right decision.

Who knows what other injustices may happen to the family while awaiting trial?

Let Cadence and Jackson pull on your heartstrings as they maneuver through obstacles and triumphs that will have you rooting for them from beginning to end. They'll show you why love is an action word through this story that's filled with mystery, suspense, and intrigue.

Available on Amazon

Also by London St. Charles

STANDALONES

The Husband We Share

Betrayal of Trust

King of Chatham

Under the Tree: Reno and Zuri's First Christmas

30 Days of Pleasure (2021)

Queen of the Gold Coast (2021)

ANTHOLOGIES

Sugar

Just One Kiss

Evanescence (2022)

CASTLE SERIES

Kings of the Castle (collaboration)

DECEPTION SERIES

Sugarcoated Deception

Deadly Deception

UNEXPECTED SERIES

Embracing the Unexpected (January 2021)

Chasing the Unexpected (Summer 2021)

Claiming the Unexpected (Winter 2021)